REBEL GiRLS

REBEL GiRLS COOK

100+ KID-TESTED RECIPES YOU CAN MAKE, SHARE + ENJOY!

TEN SPEED PRESS
California | New York

CONTENTS

Hi, Rebels!

Welcome to the first-ever Rebel Girls cookbook. We're so glad you're here.

Whether you're totally new to cooking or already whipping up meals with your family, you're in the right place. Do you want to know the best way to pit an avocado or crack an egg? Get step-by-step instructions that will make tricky techniques a breeze. Are you curious about different cuisines? Explore international recipes and ingredients full of fun flavors. Are you a picky eater? Take a chance on some recipes you've never tried, prepared just the way you like them—by you!

No matter who you are, *Rebel Girls Cook* will teach you important cooking skills, introduce you to new foods and recipes, and give you the confidence to conquer the kitchen. Trying new things is one of the best ways to boost your confidence. You'll feel like a star chef in no time!

We'll introduce you to some cooking basics before we dive into the recipes to make sure you feel comfortable in the kitchen. You'll find delicious recipes from all kinds of cuisines in each chapter. Along the way, you'll learn fun facts about women from history (both in and out of the kitchen), hear from kids like you about their favorite recipes, and ponder questions that will make you think about the wonderful world of cooking.

You'll also meet some of the Rebels currently ruling the food world. These chefs have opened their own restaurants, published cookbooks, and shared their cuisines with people around the globe. In *Rebel Girls Cook*, they'll share their advice—and their recipes—with you. Asma Khan, owner of Darjeeling Express restaurant in London, will teach you to make a fish kabab. Rahanna Bisseret Martinez, who competed on *Top Chef Junior*, will show you how to craft mushroom onigiri. And food writer and cookbook author Hetty Lui McKinnon will help you whip up some sheet pan chow mein. These are just a few of the amazing women you'll meet in these pages. We hope they'll inspire you to forge your own path, whether you want to become a chef one day or are looking for creative ways to express yourself through food.

We can't wait for you to discover new flavors, show off your skills with your friends and family, and decide how you want to run your kitchen. Let's get cooking!

—THE REBEL GIRLS TEAM

WELCOME TO THE KITCHEN: HOW TO USE THIS BOOK

GETTING STARTED

You've picked out a recipe and you're ready to start cooking. But before you pull out ingredients or heat the oven, **read the entire recipe!** Read it from start to finish. (And then maybe read it one more time.) This way you know what to expect, how involved the recipe is, and when you might need to ask a grown-up for support. Pay attention to the kitchen equipment you'll need to have on hand—it's **in special blue text** throughout each recipe.

Once you've read through the entire recipe, it's time to **prep your ingredients**. First things first: Definitely wash your hands, and tie back your hair if it's long and getting in your way. Measure out ingredients using dry measuring cups, a liquid measuring cup, or measuring spoons. Chop veggies, fruits, and herbs (always wash and dry them first!). Putting each prepped ingredient in its own bowl helps you stay organized.

Now it's time to cook! Follow the recipe steps, one at a time. Check out the step-by-step photos, if the recipe has them. Be sure to ask a grown-up for help whenever using anything sharp (like a knife or a food processor) or hot (like the stovetop or oven).

And remember, if your final dish doesn't quite turn out the way you hoped, don't sweat it. Mistakes are a normal part of cooking and baking—and a great way to learn. Think about what you'd do differently next time. Even if your food isn't perfect, we bet it still tastes great!

DECODING RECIPES

You'll see different symbols throughout this book—these will give you important information about each recipe. Here's what they mean.

 This part of the recipe is a little dangerous. Ask a grown-up for help before proceeding.

 Recipe takes less than 30 minutes to make.

 Recipe doesn't require the use of the stovetop, oven, or toaster.

 Recipe doesn't require the use of a knife or food processor.

 Recipe is a project, or is more involved—great for weekends, vacations, and cooking together with family or friends.

 Recipe is vegetarian, or does not contain any meat, poultry, or fish, but might include eggs.

 Recipe is vegan or does not contain any animal products.

 Recipe can be customized, just the way you like it.

KiTCHEN BASiCS

These essential techniques show up in many recipes in this book . . . and beyond! Practice them now and you'll be ready to tackle just about any recipe you come across.

!! Many of the techniques in this section use a chef's knife or a paring knife. Always ask a grown-up for help when working with knives.

HOW TO MEASURE WET AND DRY iNGREDiENTS

Wet Ingredients
Use a liquid measuring cup to measure wet ingredients, such as water or milk. Slowly add your liquid to the measuring cup until it reaches the correct line, such as ¼ cup, ⅓ cup, or 2 cups. Bend down and get eye level with the measuring cup. Make sure the level of the liquid lines up with the measurement line.

Dry Ingredients
Use dry measuring cups to measure dry ingredients, such as flour and granulated sugar. Dip your measuring cup into your ingredient, making sure to fill it completely (it's OK if there is more than you need). Swipe the flat back of a butter knife across the top of the measuring cup to push away the excess ingredient.

MEASURiNG SPOONS

Use measuring spoons to measure small amounts of liquid or dry ingredients, such as oil, salt, baking powder, and spices. Most sets of measuring spoons have different spoons for 1 tablespoon, 1 teaspoon, ½ teaspoon, and ¼ teaspoon.

HOW TO HOLD A CHEF'S KNiFE

To keep your fingers safe, it's important to hold a knife the right way! Wrap your hand around the knife's handle and grip the top part of the blade closest to the handle between your pointer finger and thumb. As you slice or chop, always hold the food with your other hand in a "bear claw"—that means tuck your fingertips under, which keeps them safely away from the sharp knife.

HOW TO CHOP FRESH HERBS

If your recipe calls for just the leaves, pick them off the stems before chopping. Put the leaves (and stems, if using) in a pile on a cutting board. Hold a chef's knife with one hand on the knife's handle and the other hand flat on top of the knife blade. Rock the knife back and forth to chop the leaves into small pieces, moving the knife side to side as you chop.

HOW TO PEEL AND CHOP ONIONS

1

Place the onion on a cutting board. Use a chef's knife to cut the onion in half through the root. Lay each half flat-side down on the cutting board and trim off the nonroot ends. Use your fingers to remove the peels. Discard the peels and trimmed ends.

2

Use the chef's knife to make vertical cuts from the trimmed end almost to the root end of the onion, ¼ to ½ inch apart.

3

Turn the onion and slice it across the cuts you just made. These cuts should also be ¼ to ½ inch apart.

HOW TO PREP CHILES

It's a good idea to wear disposable gloves—and avoid touching your face—when working with chiles. Capsaicin, the compound that makes chiles spicy, can irritate your skin.

1

Place the chile on a **cutting board**. Use a **chef's knife** to slice off the stem and very top of the chile. Discard the stem.

2

Cut the chile in half the long way.

3

Use a **small spoon** to scoop out and discard the seeds.

4

Place one chile half skin-side down. Slice it the long way into thin strips. Then slice it the short way into very small pieces. Repeat with the other chile half, depending on how much your recipe calls for.

REBEL GiRLS COOK

HOW TO PEEL AND CHOP OR MINCE GARLIC

1

Place a garlic clove on a cutting board. Use the flat bottom of a dry measuring cup to press down on the garlic clove. Peel off and throw away the papery skin.

2

Hold a chef's knife with one hand on the knife's handle and the other hand flat on top of the knife blade. Rock the knife back and forth to chop the garlic into small pieces, moving the knife side to side as you chop. For minced garlic, keep cutting until you have very tiny pieces of garlic.

HOW TO PIT AN AVOCADO

1

Use a butter knife to cut the avocado in half lengthwise (the long way), going all the way around the pit in the middle. Twist the two halves of the avocado in opposite directions and pull to separate them.

2

Pick up the avocado half that has the pit in it. Place your thumbs behind the pit on the outside and press with your thumbs to pop the pit out (be careful, it might go flying!). Discard the pit.

HOW TO ZEST AND JUICE CITRUS FRUITS

TO ZEST

Zest is the colorful peel on lemons, limes, oranges, and other citrus fruits. To remove it, gently rub the fruit back and forth on a rasp grater (also called a Microplane). Keep turning the fruit so you remove just the colorful skin, not the white layer underneath.

TO JUICE

Use a chef's knife to cut the fruit in half the short way. Place one half in a citrus juicer. Hold the juicer over a small bowl and squeeze—the juice will drain into the bowl. Repeat as needed.

HOW TO GRATE AND SHRED CHEESE

TO SHRED

Rub a large piece of cheese back and forth across the large holes of a box grater— keep your hand away from the sharp holes! You typically shred softer cheeses, such as mozzarella or cheddar.

TO GRATE

Rub a large piece of cheese back and forth on the small holes of a box grater or a rasp grater—keep your hand away from the sharp holes! You typically grate hard cheeses, such as Parmesan or pecorino.

HOW TO MELT BUTTER

On the stovetop: Place the butter in a small saucepan over low heat. Cook, swirling the saucepan occasionally, until the butter is melted. Turn off the stovetop and slide the saucepan to a cool burner.

In the microwave: Use a butter knife to cut the butter into 1-tablespoon pieces. Place the butter in a microwave-safe bowl and cover it with a microwave-safe plate. Heat it in the microwave at 50 percent power until the butter is melted, checking every 30 seconds.

HOW TO CRACK AND SEPARATE EGGS

To crack: Gently tap the flatter side of an egg on a flat surface. Pull the shell apart over a bowl, letting the egg yolk and egg white fall into the bowl. Discard the shell. Wash your hands when finished.

To separate the yolk and the white: Use your hand to very gently scoop up the yolk. Hold your hand over the bowl, letting any extra white fall through your fingers. Place the yolk in a second bowl. Wash your hands when finished.

HOW TO SEASON TO TASTE

When a recipe tells you to season to taste, that usually means adding a small amount of salt (and sometimes ground black pepper). Taste your dish. Do you think it could use a little more salt and/or pepper? Add a tiny bit, stir, and taste again with a clean fork or spoon. What do you think? Repeat until the dish tastes well seasoned to you.

HOW TO USE AN INSTANT-READ THERMOMETER

A thermometer is the best way to tell when meat or fish has reached a safe temperature to eat. Insert the pointy end of an instant-read thermometer into the middle of the thickest part of the meat or fish. (Sometimes it's easiest to use tongs to hold the meat or fish in place while you do this.) Read the temperature and compare it to the temperature the recipe says the food should be—keep cooking as needed!

WHAT'S THE DIFFERENCE BETWEEN HOT OIL AND SMOKING OIL?

In many recipes in this book, you'll see instructions to heat oil in a skillet on the stovetop until it's hot but not smoking. To tell the difference, get eye level with the pan (but keep your face a good distance away!). If you see tiny little waves on the surface of the oil, it's hot and ready for you to start cooking. If you see wisps of smoke coming off the oil, it's smoking and it's too hot. Turn off the stovetop, slide the skillet to a cool burner, and let the oil cool for a few minutes. Ask a grown-up to wipe out the skillet. Then start again with fresh oil.

PARTY TIME!
TIPS AND IDEAS FOR DELICIOUS CELEBRATIONS

A special dish or dessert is a great way to make any celebration—or even a regular Tuesday night—feel memorable. Try some of these fun ideas for how to make cooking and eating with family and friends extra special.

SUNDAE BAR

Make a batch or two of Banana "Ice Cream" (page 222) and set up a sundae bar! Put toppings in a muffin tin or small bowls for easy access, make a batch of whipped cream (see page 220) as well as Hot Fudge Sauce (page 228) and/or Strawberry Sauce (page 229), and let everyone build their own sundae. Don't forget the cherries!

POPCORN PARTY

When it's time for movie night, pop a batch or two of popcorn (see page 100). Let everyone add their own spices, seasonings, and toppings to create a bowl of popcorn, just the way they like it. You could even host a taste test to determine which flavor is the family favorite.

DECORATE THE TABLE

If you're having family dinner, set the table early (before you start cooking) and make it look nice. Add a tablecloth. Make a centerpiece with fresh flowers, fruits and vegetables, seashells, or other interesting objects from around the house. Pick a color scheme inspired by what you're serving. You could even design menus to put at each place setting.

COOK TOGETHER

Make preparing the food part of the party! Set up a few workstations around the table or kitchen counter and have everyone help make dumplings (page 113), Spam Musubi (page 109), or Mushroom Onigiri (page 77). Or, if you're feeling sweet, let everyone decorate their own Chocolate Cupcakes (see page 204) with Vanilla Buttercream Frosting (page 205), sprinkles, sanding sugar, and/or crushed cookies or candies.

BREAKFAST FOR DINNER

Who says you can only eat breakfast foods in the morning? One-Bowl Fluffy Pancakes (page 36), Classic French Toast (page 38), Menemen (page 29), and Cháo Gà (page 55) can serve the whole family—and everyone can customize their meal with different toppings or sauces. You could even wear your pajamas while you eat!

BREAKFAST

FRiED EGGS

You'll need a nonstick skillet with a tight-fitting lid for this recipe. If you have a glass lid, that makes it easy to see when the yolks are cooked to your liking. There's no need to flip these eggs—the hot steam trapped by the lid cooks the tops of the eggs, while the hot skillet cooks the bottoms.

INGREDIENTS

2 large eggs

Salt and pepper

1 tablespoon water

1 tablespoon unsalted butter

1. Carefully crack each egg into its own **small bowl** or **mug**, keeping the yolk intact. (If you break the yolk, don't worry! You could beat and scramble that egg [see page 29] instead of frying it, or save it in the fridge for another use.) Sprinkle each egg with a little bit of salt and pepper.

2. Measure the water into another **small bowl** and set it next to the stove.

3. Add the butter to a **10- or 12-inch nonstick skillet**. Heat the skillet on the stovetop over medium-high heat until the butter is fully melted and beginning to bubble and sizzle, 1 to 3 minutes.

!! 4. Pick up the handle of the skillet and carefully swirl the melted butter so it evenly coats the pan. Set the skillet back down on the stovetop.

5. Pour the eggs into the skillet, keeping space between them. (If they run into each other, no big deal! You can separate them with a spatula once they're cooked.)

6. Reduce the heat to medium. Cook until the whites are set and beginning to brown at the edges, 1 to 2 minutes.

7. Carefully pour the water into an empty spot in the skillet (it may sputter and pop) and quickly put on the lid to trap the steam. Cook for about 1 minute for runny yolks or about 2 minutes 30 seconds for firm yolks. Turn off the stovetop and slide the skillet to a cool burner.

8. Use **oven mitts** to remove the lid. (Keep your face away from the skillet—hot steam will escape when you remove the lid!) Use a spatula to transfer the eggs to **serving plates**. Serve warm.

FUN FOOD FACT

Pakistani activist Malala Yousafzai's family always had fried eggs for breakfast. You might be used to eating yours with toast, but Malala had hers with chapatis, yummy flatbreads made from flour, ghee (clarified butter), and water. It's a meal fit for a Nobel Peace Prize winner!

EGGS YOUR WAY:
SOFT-BOILED OR HARD-BOILED

INGREDIENTS

1 to 6 large eggs, cold
from the fridge

Salt and pepper

Toast sticks (optional)

Soft- and hard-boiled eggs are both cooked *in* their shells. The only difference is the amount of time they cook. Soft-boiled eggs have runny yolks, while hard-boiled eggs are solid throughout. It's important to cook the eggs for exactly the time stated in the recipe, so get your timer ready in advance! You can make up to six eggs using this recipe—the timing and amount of water will stay the same.

1 Fill a **medium saucepan** with water until the water is about ½ inch deep. Bring the water to a boil on the stovetop over medium-high heat.

2 Use **tongs** to gently place the eggs into the boiling water. (The water will come about halfway up the sides of the eggs—they won't be fully covered!)

3 Cover the saucepan with a lid and cook for exactly 6 minutes 30 seconds for soft-boiled eggs or 13 minutes for hard-boiled eggs. (You should see steam coming out from under the lid of the saucepan—if the lid is rattling, turn the heat down to medium.)

4 While the eggs are cooking, fill a **medium bowl** with ice cubes and 2 cups of cold water. Set this ice bath next to the stove.

5 When the eggs are ready, turn off the stovetop and slide the saucepan to a cool burner. Use **oven mitts** to remove the saucepan lid. (Keep your face away from the saucepan—hot steam will escape when you remove the lid!) Use tongs to gently transfer the eggs to the ice bath. Go to step 6 for soft-boiled eggs. Go to step 8 for hard-boiled eggs.

6 **For soft-boiled eggs:** Let the eggs chill in the ice bath for 1 minute (this stops them from continuing to cook, but they'll still be warm inside). Use the tongs to remove the eggs from the ice bath and pat them dry with a **kitchen towel**.

7 To serve, use the side of a small spoon to crack the shell in a circle around the top of the egg, then scoop across to remove the top piece of shell. (You will use the rest of the shell as a little bowl from which you can eat your egg.) Sprinkle the white

and yolk inside with a little bit of salt and pepper, and scoop the egg out of its shell with a spoon (or toast sticks) as you eat.

8   **For hard-boiled eggs:** Let the eggs chill in the ice bath for 15 minutes (this stops them from continuing to cook and cools them to room temperature). Use tongs to remove them from the ice bath, pat them dry with a kitchen towel, and then serve them or transfer them to an airtight container and refrigerate for up to 1 week.

9   To serve, gently tap the egg on the counter to break the shell all over. Starting at the wider end of the egg, begin to peel off the shell and the membrane underneath. Hold the egg under cold running water in the sink and peel off the rest of the shell and membrane. Discard the shell and pat the egg dry with a paper towel. Sprinkle the egg with a little bit of salt and pepper before you eat.

HARD-
BOILED

SOFT-
BOILED

📢 FUN FOOD FACT

When Amelia Earhart flew solo from Mexico City to New York, she ate mostly hard-boiled eggs. Small, self-contained, and easy to eat in her cramped cockpit, they kept her fueled up for her sixteen-hour journey. How many eggs would you need to last you sixteen hours?

When Ana was growing up in the Pacific Northwest, she would follow her grandma around the kitchen as she baked rolls and churned fresh, creamy butter. Whenever her mom baked, Ana was always right behind her, too, looking for beaters and bowls to lick any leftover batter from.

These days, Ana's not following anyone around the kitchen—she's running her own! She's the owner and executive chef at Oleana Restaurant and Sofra Bakery and Cafe, and she co-owns the restaurant Sarma as well. On a trip to Turkey, she became fascinated with the variety of dishes and flavors and brought them back to her Boston-area restaurants.

As a child, Ana thought she didn't like vegetables because she usually had them frozen or from a can. But when she tried fresh veggies from the farmer's market cooked in butter and oil, she fell in love. Now vegetables are some of her favorite things to cook—usually with lots of flavorful spices.

Her proudest accomplishment is raising her daughter while cofounding her food businesses. She says, "I love the fact that I showed her how wonderful it is to have a job that fulfills you and makes others very happy."

Ana's favorite person to cook with: "One of our longtime chefs at Oleana, Paige Lombardi. She and I cooked many meals together, and it was always fun to work with her."

If Ana could invite any Rebel to dinner, she'd pick Oprah, and she would cook manti, a type of Turkish dumpling often served with yogurt, tomato, brown butter, and spices.

MENEMEN
TURKISH SCRAMBLED EGGS WITH TOMATOES AND PEPPERS

"Menemen is a Turkish dish of scrambled eggs with lots of fresh tomato and sweet and hot peppers. It's best eaten when garden-fresh tomatoes are in season—otherwise, look for red plum tomatoes or good-quality greenhouse vine tomatoes. I love to serve menemen with lightly toasted or steamed pita, string cheese, sliced cucumber, and a few olives to create a complete Turkish breakfast experience." —Ana Sortun

INGREDIENTS

8 large eggs

½ teaspoon kosher salt or sea salt

3 greenhouse or beefsteak tomatoes

2 tablespoons unsalted butter or extra-virgin olive oil

1 cup finely chopped green or red bell pepper (about 1 medium pepper)

2 tablespoons finely chopped jalapeño chile or Hungarian wax pepper (about ½ chile, see page 12)

1 scallion, root end trimmed, thinly sliced

2 teaspoons tomato paste

4 (7-inch) pitas, or 4 slices toast

Sliced cucumber, olives, and/or string cheese, for serving (optional)

1. Crack the eggs into a large bowl. Add the salt and whisk until the yolks and whites are just combined.

2. Place the tomatoes on a cutting board. Use a chef's knife to cut each tomato in half through the equator (not through the root end). Squeeze or spoon out most of the seeds and discard.

3. Place a box grater over a shallow dish. Keeping your hand flat, carefully grate the cut side of each tomato half on the large holes of the grater. Stop when your hand gets close to the holes, leaving the tomato skin in one piece. Discard the skins.

4. Add the butter to a large nonstick skillet. Heat the skillet on the stovetop over medium heat until the butter is melted. Add the bell pepper, jalapeño, and scallion and cook, stirring occasionally with a rubber spatula, until the peppers are tender, about 5 minutes.

5. Add the grated tomato and tomato paste and season with salt to taste (see page 17). Cook until the sauce thickens slightly, 3 to 5 minutes.

6. Add the eggs and gently stir them into the sauce.

7. Cook, stirring gently, until the eggs are scrambled to your liking, about 2 minutes for very soft set eggs or about 4 minutes for firmer eggs. Turn off the stovetop.

8. Spread the egg mixture on the pitas or toast. Serve warm, with sliced cucumber, olives, and string cheese (if using).

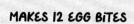

MUFFIN TIN EGG BITES

INGREDIENTS

Vegetable oil spray

8 large eggs

½ teaspoon Dijon mustard (optional)

1½ cups shredded cheddar cheese (see page 16)

½ teaspoon table salt

¼ teaspoon black pepper

4 slices cooked bacon (see page 51), chopped (about ½ cup)

½ cup chopped bell pepper

12 tater tots, thawed

Our mini egg bites have a special surprise in the center—a tater tot! It's important to use liners in your muffin tin for this recipe—otherwise, the egg mixture will stick. Paper cupcake liners, parchment paper liners, silicone liners, or even parchment paper cut into 4-inch squares will work. If your muffin tin is made of silicone, there's no need to line it—the egg bites will pop right out. Any color bell pepper works in this recipe.

1 Set an oven rack in the middle position and heat the oven to 350°F. Line a **12-cup muffin tin** with your choice of **liners** (see the introduction). Spray the inside of each liner with vegetable oil spray.

2 In a **large bowl**, **whisk** the eggs, mustard (if using), cheese, salt, and black pepper until well combined.

3 Use a **liquid measuring cup** or **ladle** to divide the egg mixture evenly among the muffin cups (they should be about halfway full). Sprinkle the bacon and bell pepper evenly over the egg mixture in each muffin cup. Press one tater tot into the center of each muffin cup (see the photo on the opposite page).

4 Place the muffin tin in the oven. Bake until the egg bites have set (turned solid) and risen over the rims of the muffin cups, 20 to 25 minutes.

‼5 Use **oven mitts** to remove the muffin tin from the oven and place it on the stovetop or a **cooling rack**. Let the egg bites cool slightly, about 5 minutes.

6 Use a **butter knife** or **chopstick** to carefully remove the egg bites from the muffin tin (be careful, the muffin tin will still be hot!). Serve warm.

SPINACH & FETA MUFFIN TIN EGG BITES

Use 1 cup chopped baby spinach instead of the bacon and bell pepper. Use crumbled feta cheese instead of the shredded cheddar. In step 2, whisk all the ingredients except the tater tots together. In step 3, skip the sprinkling and just press the tater tots into the egg mixture after filling the cups.

YOU'RE THE CHEF

"The pop of salty potato in the middle was such a fun surprise to my mouth!"
—Anastasia, age 9

EGG & CHEESE BREAKFAST TACOS

These clever little "smash" tacos mean you can cook a fried egg right into your tortilla! Any melty cheese will work here—cheddar, Monterey Jack, American, Swiss—use what you've got. Add your favorite toppings to your finished tacos: chopped tomatoes, cooked bacon or sausage, avocado, hot sauce, and salsa are all delicious.

1   Carefully crack each egg into its own **small bowl** or **mug**, keeping the yolk intact. Sprinkle each egg with a little bit of salt and pepper. Set both near the stove.

2   Add the oil to a **12-inch nonstick skillet**. Heat the skillet on the stovetop over medium heat until the oil is hot but not smoking (see page 17), about 2 minutes.

!! 3   Using **oven mitts**, pick up the handle of the skillet and carefully swirl the oil so it evenly coats the pan. Set the skillet back down on the stovetop.

4   Carefully pour the eggs, one at a time, onto opposite sides of the skillet. If you like your egg yolk runny, try to keep it whole. If you don't, use the corner of a spatula to break the yolk so it will cook all the way through.

5   Cook the eggs for 2 minutes. Use a **spatula** to flip over each egg. Carefully lay one slice of cheese on top of each egg or sprinkle each egg with 2 tablespoons of grated cheese. Cover the skillet with a **lid** and cook for 1 minute.

6   Use oven mitts to carefully remove the lid. (The cheese should be melted now–if it's not, put the lid back on and cook for another 30 seconds.) Carefully place 1 tortilla on top of the melted cheese on each egg.

!! 7   Slide the spatula completely underneath one of the eggs. Carefully place your fingertips on top of the tortilla. Lift the spatula and flip the taco over, moving your fingers out of the way as you flip. Repeat with the second taco.

8   Cook the tacos until the tortillas have warmed through, about 1 minute. Turn off the stovetop. Use the spatula to transfer the tacos to **serving plates**. Season to taste.

INGREDIENTS

2 large eggs

Salt and pepper

1 teaspoon vegetable oil

2 slices cheese (see the introduction), or 4 tablespoons grated cheese (see page 16)

2 (6-inch) corn tortillas

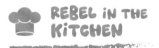

REBEL IN THE KITCHEN

Today, it's easy to grab a pack of tortillas from the store, but traditionally, making tortillas was a woman's job, and it wasn't an easy one. Indigenous women in Mexico would grind soaked, specially treated corn. Then they would press it into round, flat shapes and cook it over a fire. Some chefs, like Rosalía Chay Chuc, are keeping tradition alive by making tortillas the old way. She serves her cochinita pibil, a type of slow-roasted pork, in homemade tortillas at her restaurant in Yucatán, Mexico.

TOFU SCRAMBLE

SERVES 4

INGREDIENTS

1 (16-ounce) block firm or extra-firm tofu

2 tablespoons olive oil

¾ teaspoon ground turmeric

½ teaspoon table salt

¼ teaspoon pepper

1 tablespoon nutritional yeast (optional)

This super-simple vegan breakfast scramble gets its bright yellow color from turmeric, a spice in the ginger family, and its delicious nutty, cheesy flavor from nutritional yeast, savory flakes of yeast (not the kind you use to bake bread) available in most grocery stores. You can also add stir-ins to your scramble, such as roasted vegetables, herbs, cooked greens, or cooked vegan sausage. Add them at the end of step 6 and cook for 2 or 3 minutes longer to let all the ingredients warm through. You can serve your scramble with toast or tortillas.

1 Line a **dinner plate** with three layers of **paper towels**. Use a **chef's knife** to cut the block of tofu in half the long way. Lay the tofu slabs on the paper towels and let them drain for at least 10 minutes.

2 Place the drained tofu in a **medium bowl** and use a **fork** or a **potato masher** to break it up into small crumbles. (Or crumble the tofu with your hands.)

3 Add the oil to a **10-inch nonstick skillet**. Heat the skillet on the stovetop over medium heat until the oil is hot but not smoking (see page 17), about 1 minute.

!!4 Using **oven mitts**, pick up the handle of the skillet and carefully swirl the oil so it evenly coats the pan. Set the skillet back down on the stovetop.

5 Sprinkle the turmeric over the oil and cook, stirring occasionally with a **wooden spoon** or **rubber spatula**, for about 30 seconds.

6 Add the tofu crumbles, salt, pepper, and nutritional yeast (if using) and cook, stirring occasionally, until the tofu is warmed through and just beginning to brown, 5 to 7 minutes. (If you're adding any additional ingredients, do so now, and cook for 2 to 3 minutes longer.) Turn off the stovetop.

7 Carefully transfer the scramble to **serving plates**. Serve.

SOUTHWEST TOFU SCRAMBLE

In step 5, add ½ teaspoon chili powder and ½ teaspoon ground cumin to the skillet with the turmeric. In step 6, add ¼ cup chopped bell pepper and ¼ cup chopped onion to the skillet and cook for 2 minutes before adding the tofu crumbles and other ingredients. After the tofu mixture has cooked for 5 to 7 minutes, add 1 cup of drained and rinsed black beans to the skillet and cook until the beans are warmed through, 2 to 3 minutes.

 ## REBEL IN THE KITCHEN

Growing up in Japan, author Akiko Aoyagi always ate tofu. It is high in protein, doesn't cost much, and is made from plants, making it a great way to feed all kinds of people. Plus, it's delicious! When she learned that tofu wasn't as popular in other parts of the world, she set out to change that. She and her partner, William Shurtleff, wrote cookbooks, gave talks, and spread the word. Thanks to them, many more people know the magic of tofu.

ONE-BOWL FLUFFY PANCAKES

INGREDIENTS

2 cups all-purpose flour

¼ cup granulated sugar

4 teaspoons baking powder

1 teaspoon table salt

⅛ teaspoon ground cinnamon (optional)

1½ cups milk

2 large eggs

2 tablespoons vegetable oil, plus more for cooking

¼ teaspoon vanilla extract

These pancakes are fast, fluffy, and don't make a *huge* mess of your kitchen. You can serve each batch of pancakes as you make them, or you can keep finished pancakes warm while you're cooking the rest: Place them on oven-safe plates, an oven-safe platter, or a baking sheet in a 200°F oven. Make sure to use oven mitts to take them out of the oven when you're ready to serve (the plates, platter, or baking sheet will be hot). Serve with extra butter and maple syrup, a dusting of confectioners' (powdered) sugar, or drizzled with Strawberry Sauce (page 229).

1   In a **large bowl**, **whisk** together the flour, sugar, baking powder, salt, and cinnamon (if using).

2   Add the milk, eggs, oil, and vanilla. Use the whisk to break the egg yolks, then whisk until the ingredients are just combined and the eggs are evenly distributed but the batter is still a little lumpy. Let the batter sit for 10 minutes to thicken up.

3   Add ½ teaspoon of oil to a **12-inch nonstick skillet**. Heat the skillet on the stovetop over medium heat until the oil is hot but not smoking (see page 17), 2 to 3 minutes.

!!4   Using **oven mitts**, pick up the handle of the skillet and carefully swirl the oil so it evenly coats the pan. Set the skillet back down on the stovetop.

5   Use a **¼-cup dry measuring cup** to scoop 3 portions of batter into the skillet, leaving some space between them, then use the measuring cup to spread each portion into a circle. If you're adding fillings (see Pancake Add-Ins), sprinkle them evenly over each pancake while the batter is still wet.

6   Cook the pancakes until bubbles pop on the surface and the bottoms are golden brown (slide a **spatula** underneath a pancake and lift up a little bit to peek underneath to check), 2 to 3 minutes.

7   Use the spatula to flip each pancake. Cook until the second side of each pancake is golden brown, 1 to 2 minutes. (If your pancakes start to get too dark too quickly, turn the heat down a little bit.)

FUN FOOD FACT

You can add all kinds of mix-ins and flavors to a basic pancake recipe. Famous freedom fighter Rosa Parks swore by a pancake recipe that used peanut butter!

8 Use the spatula to transfer the pancakes to serving plates (to keep them warm, see the introduction). Repeat steps 5 to 7 with the remaining batter, adding ½ teaspoon oil to the skillet and swirling it to coat the pan evenly in between batches—you'll make 4 or 5 batches total. When you're done with your last batch, turn off the stovetop. Serve.

PANCAKE ADD-INS

After adding the batter to the pan in step 5, sprinkle each pancake with 1 tablespoon of fresh or frozen blueberries, 1 tablespoon of regular or mini chocolate chips, or 3 or 4 slices of banana.

CLASSIC FRENCH TOAST

INGREDIENTS

8 slices sandwich bread

4 large eggs

3 tablespoons granulated sugar

⅛ teaspoon pumpkin pie spice or apple pie spice

Pinch of table salt

1⅓ cups milk

¼ teaspoon vanilla extract

2 tablespoons unsalted butter

This is a flexible French toast recipe. You can use sandwich bread, but feel free to use thicker-cut bread, such as challah, brioche, or Texas toast, instead. If you use a thicker-cut bread, increase the baking time in step 2 to 15 minutes and the soaking time in step 5 to 30 seconds per side to make sure the custard soaks all the way to the middle of the bread. Don't use crusty loaves, such as sourdough in this recipe—a soft, squishy bread is best. Pumpkin pie spice and apple pie spice, which contain cinnamon and other warm spices— nutmeg, ginger, allspice, and/or cloves—taste great with French toast, but if you don't have them on hand, you can use a pinch of cinnamon and a pinch of nutmeg instead.

Serve with extra butter and maple syrup, a dusting of confectioners' (powdered) sugar, and/or a drizzle of Strawberry Sauce (page 229).

1   Set an oven rack in the middle position and heat the oven to 200°F. Place a cooling rack on top of a rimmed baking sheet.

2   Spread out the bread slices on top of the cooling rack. When the oven is ready, place the baking sheet in the oven and bake until the surface of the bread is dried out, about 10 minutes.

3   While the bread is baking, in a shallow dish, whisk the eggs, sugar, pumpkin pie spice, and salt until the yolks and whites are well combined. Add the milk and vanilla and whisk until well combined and smooth. This is your custard!

!!4   Use oven mitts to remove the baking sheet from the oven and place it on the stovetop or a second cooling rack (don't turn the oven off). Let the bread cool slightly, then transfer it to a second rimmed baking sheet. Use oven mitts to place the baking sheet with the cooling rack back in the oven (this is where your French toast will land to keep warm later).

5   Place 1 slice of the cooled bread into the egg mixture and hold it down for about 15 seconds. Flip it over and hold it down again for another 15 seconds, until the custard soaks into the middle of the

CONTINUED

bread. Gently lift the bread and let the extra custard drip back into the dish, then place the soaked bread back on the baking sheet. Repeat to soak the remaining bread slices with custard. Wash your hands and discard any extra custard when you are done.

6   Use a **butter knife** to cut each tablespoon of butter in half (you'll have 4 pieces total).

7   Add 1 piece of the butter to a **12-inch nonstick skillet**. Heat the skillet on the stovetop over medium heat until the butter is melted and the skillet is hot, 2 to 3 minutes.

‼ 8   Using an **oven mitt**, pick up the handle of the skillet and carefully swirl the melted butter so it evenly coats the pan. Set the skillet back down on the stovetop.

9   Use a **spatula** to transfer 2 of the soaked bread slices to the skillet. Cook until the bread is golden brown on the bottom (slide the spatula under a slice of bread and lift a little bit to peek underneath to check), 2 to 4 minutes.

10   Use the spatula to flip each piece of bread. Cook until the second side of each piece is golden brown, 2 to 4 minutes. (If your French toast starts to get too dark too quickly, turn the heat down a little bit.)

‼ 11   Use the spatula to transfer the French toast to the baking sheet with the cooling rack in the oven. Repeat steps 7 to 10 in three more batches with the remaining soaked bread. When you're done with your last batch, turn off the stovetop.

12   Use oven mitts to remove the baking sheet from the oven and place it on the stovetop or a cooling rack. Serve the French toast warm.

 **FUN FOOD FACT**

The first French toast recipe dates back to the fifth century, and it's not from France—it's from the Roman Empire. Roman Rebels like Hortensia, the famous orator, may have enjoyed bread soaked in milk and egg, fried, and topped with honey.

CHOCOLATE-HAZELNUT SWIRL BANANA BREAD

MAKES 1 LOAF

Very ripe bananas have heavily speckled black or brown skins and very soft flesh. If your loaf pan measures 8½ by 4½ inches, your banana bread will take a little longer to bake—start checking it closer to the end of the time range. If your pan measures 9 by 5 inches, your banana bread will bake faster, so start checking it closer to the beginning of the time range. We used Nutella in this recipe, but any similar chocolate-hazelnut spread should work.

1. Set an oven rack in the middle position and heat the oven to 350°F. Spray the inside of a **metal** or **glass loaf pan** with vegetable oil spray.

2. Place the bananas in a **large bowl**. Use a **potato masher** or a **fork** to mash the bananas until they're broken down but not all the way smooth. Add the sugar, eggs, oil, milk, and vanilla and **whisk** until well combined.

3. Add the flour, baking soda, and salt and use a **rubber spatula** to gently stir until all the ingredients are just combined and there's no more dry flour (make sure to scrape along the bottom and sides of the bowl as you stir—more dry flour might be hiding there).

4. Add the chocolate-hazelnut spread to a **medium microwave-safe bowl**. Heat it in the microwave until it's loosened up (you can shake the bowl to check), 15 to 30 seconds.

5. Use a **½-cup dry measuring cup** to scoop ½ cup of the banana bread batter into the bowl with the chocolate-hazelnut spread. Whisk until well combined.

6. Add half of the plain batter to the greased loaf pan and use the rubber spatula to spread it into an even layer. Use a **spoon** to dollop half of the chocolate-hazelnut batter onto the plain batter in the pan.

INGREDIENTS

Vegetable oil spray

3 very ripe bananas, peeled

¾ cup granulated sugar

2 large eggs

⅓ cup vegetable oil

¼ cup milk

1 teaspoon vanilla extract

2 cups all-purpose flour

1 teaspoon baking soda

½ teaspoon table salt

½ cup chocolate-hazelnut spread

2 tablespoons chopped hazelnuts (optional)

CONTINUED

CHOCOLATE-HAZELNUT SWIRL BANANA BREAD
CONTINUED

7 Add the remaining plain batter on top and smooth it out with the rubber spatula. Dollop spoonfuls of the remaining chocolate-hazelnut batter on top of that. Use a **butter knife** or **chopstick** to swirl the batters together. Sprinkle the top evenly with the hazelnuts (if using).

8 Place the loaf pan in the oven and bake until a **toothpick** inserted into the center of the bread comes out mostly clean, with just a few moist crumbs attached, 1 hour to 1 hour 15 minutes.

!! 9 Use **oven mitts** to remove the loaf pan from the oven and place it on a **cooling rack**. Let the bread cool in the pan for 15 minutes.

10 Use oven mitts to turn the loaf pan on its side and carefully remove the banana bread from the pan (be careful, the pan and the bread will still be hot—if the banana bread sticks, use a butter knife to gently loosen it from the sides of the loaf pan). Turn the bread upright and let it continue to cool on the cooling rack for at least 1 hour. Slice and serve warm or at room temperature.

 REBEL IN THE KITCHEN

Maui, Hawai'i, is known for its banana bread, made from fresh local bananas. Sandy Hueu started selling her famous loaves in 1983, and thirty years later, her daughter joined her. Their restaurant, Aunty Sandy's, is located on a long stretch of road dotted with food stands and restaurants, and it has a big sign out front that says "The Bread You've Been Driving For."

MINI GERMAN PANCAKES

Sometimes called Dutch babies, these puffy pancakes are light and crisp on the outside and custardy on the inside. Baking them in a muffin tin instead of a large skillet creates lots of adorable mini breakfast treats. Most German pancake recipes preheat the pan before adding the batter, which can be tricky and a little dangerous. Pouring the batter into a cool muffin tin and starting in a cold oven makes things easier (and safer!). Serve your German pancakes topped with a dusting of confectioners' (powdered) sugar, a scoop of jam, a drizzle of Strawberry Sauce (page 229), chopped fruit, or lemon juice and a sprinkle of granulated sugar.

INGREDIENTS

Vegetable oil spray

1 cup milk

3 large eggs

1 cup all-purpose flour

3 tablespoons granulated sugar

1 teaspoon vanilla extract

¼ teaspoon table salt

Pinch of ground nutmeg (optional)

1   Set an oven rack in the middle position, but do not turn on the oven. Spray the inside of each cup of a 12-cup muffin tin well with vegetable oil spray.

2   Combine the milk, eggs, flour, sugar, vanilla, salt, and nutmeg (if using) in a blender (be sure to add the milk and eggs first). Place the lid on the blender and hold it in place with a kitchen towel. Blend the mixture until smooth, about 1 minute. Stop the blender.

3   Divide the batter evenly among the greased muffin cups, filling each cup about two-thirds full.

4   Place the filled muffin tin in the cold oven. Heat the oven to 425°F and start your timer. Bake until the pancakes are puffy and light golden on top, 20 to 24 minutes.

!! 5   Use oven mitts to remove the muffin tin from the oven and place it on the stovetop or a cooling rack. Let the German pancakes cool slightly, about 5 minutes. (They will deflate as they cool, but that's OK! They will form cups to fill with delicious toppings.)

6   Use a butter knife to gently loosen the edges of the pancakes from the muffin tin and carefully remove the pancakes (be careful, the muffin tin will still be hot!). Serve the pancakes immediately, with the topping of your choice (see the introduction).

REBEL IN THE KITCHEN

Like tiny versions of full-size food? Monica Padman hosts a show called *Tiny Kitchen Cook-Off*, where she challenges celebrities to make miniature dishes that look—and taste—amazing.

AVOCADO TOAST

SERVES 2

INGREDIENTS

1 ripe avocado
(see page 14)

1 tablespoon extra-virgin olive oil

Juice of ½ small lemon
(see page 15)

2 slices crusty bread

Salt and pepper

For a heartier breakfast, you can top this avocado toast with a fried egg (page 22) or cooked bacon (see page 51). You can also sprinkle your finished toast with herbs, spices, and/or cheese—check out the ideas in "Turn Up Your Toast" on the opposite page for some inspiration.

1   Hold each avocado half over a **medium bowl** and squeeze the skins to release the flesh into the bowl. Discard the skins.

2   Add the oil and lemon juice to the bowl. Use a **potato masher** or a **fork** to lightly mash the mixture until the ingredients are well combined and the mixture is as chunky or smooth as you like it.

3   Toast the bread in a **toaster** until golden brown. Place each slice on a **serving plate**.

4   Use a **spoon** to divide the avocado mixture evenly between the two pieces of toast. Use the back of the spoon to spread it into an even layer. Sprinkle each piece with a little bit of salt and pepper. Serve.

 REBEL IN THE KITCHEN

Avocados have been grown in Mexico for more than 10,000 years. Indigenous people would eat them on tortillas, but it took a long time for the rest of the world to catch on. Avocado toast first started popping up on restaurant menus in Australia in the 1990s, and then chef Chloe Osborne made it popular in America in the 2000s. She was inspired by eating it as a child in Australia and put it on the menu at Café Gitane, a famous eatery in New York City.

TURN UP YOUR TOAST!

Everything Bagel Avócado Toast

Skip the salt and pepper in step 4. Top each piece of avocado toast with 1 or 2 slices of smoked salmon (optional). Sprinkle each piece with ½ teaspoon everything bagel seasoning.

Za'atar-Feta Avocado Toast

Sprinkle each piece of avocado toast evenly with ½ teaspoon za'atar and 1 tablespoon crumbled feta cheese.

YOGURT PARFAIT, YOUR WAY

INGREDIENTS

1 cup yogurt (plain or any flavor works)

1 cup chopped fruit (in bite-size pieces, if you're using blueberries, raspberries, or blackberries, you don't need to chop them)

1 cup something crunchy (granola, cereal, nuts, or anything else you can think of)

Three ingredients and a few minutes give you breakfast that's creamy, sweet, and crunchy. The best part? You can use any combination of yogurt, fruit, and crunchy topping you like. Try combinations such as vanilla yogurt with berries and your favorite cereal or coconut yogurt with chopped mango and granola. You can add a swirl of jam to your yogurt, or top your parfait with a drizzle of honey. Mix and match and get creative! You can substitute nondairy yogurt for plain yogurt.

1   Use a ¼-cup dry measuring cup to add ¼ cup of the yogurt to each of two small drinking glasses.

2   Top the yogurt in each glass with ¼ cup of the chopped fruit.

3   Top the fruit in each glass with ¼ cup of your something crunchy.

4   Repeat all three layers again in each glass. Serve.

 FUN FOOD FACT

In South Korea, yakult ajummas are women who sell yakult, a kind of sweet yogurt drink, door-to-door. When they started in the 1970s, they had to drag around heavy carts of ice, and people were suspicious of the yogurt they were selling—what if it had germs? Eventually, the vendors got refrigerated storage, and after a lot of advertising, their customers came around to the fact that yogurt is good for you (not to mention delicious). Today, 11,000 yakult ajummas make up South Korea's biggest all-women delivery service.

BACON TWO WAYS

Want to cook bacon without all the messy spatter? Here are two ways to do it: in the microwave (if you just need a few strips) or in the oven (if you're makin' bacon for a crowd). Because the size of bacon slices can vary, check your bacon often toward the end of the cooking time to be sure it doesn't burn.

INGREDIENTS

Sliced bacon

TO COOK BACON IN THE OVEN

1   Set an oven rack in the middle position, but don't turn on the oven. Line a **rimmed baking sheet** with **aluminum foil** or **parchment paper**.

2   Lay the bacon evenly on the prepared pan, making sure the slices do not touch.

3   Place the baking sheet in the oven and heat the oven to 425°F and start your timer. Bake until the bacon is browned and crispy, 20 to 25 minutes.

!! 4   Use **oven mitts** to remove the baking sheet from the oven and place it on the stovetop or a **cooling rack**.

5   Use **tongs** to carefully transfer the bacon to a **plate** lined with **paper towels**. Serve warm.

TO COOK BACON IN THE MICROWAVE

1   Line a **microwave-safe plate** with two layers of **paper towels**.

2   Lay 2 to 4 slices of bacon evenly on the paper towels, making sure the slices are not touching. Cover the bacon with another layer of paper towels.

3   Place the plate in the microwave. Microwave on high for 1 minute, then check the bacon for doneness. Continue to cook the bacon in 1-minute intervals until it is browned and crispy, 2 to 6 minutes. How long this will take depends on your microwave.

!! 4   Use **oven mitts** to remove the plate from the microwave and set it on the stovetop or a **cooling rack**. Serve.

REBEL IN THE KITCHEN

Nurse Florence Nightingale took care of soldiers on battlefields and in hospitals. She not only made sure her wounded patients were treated so they wouldn't get sick, she also made sure they were well fed. In 1861, she published a cookbook about how to cook for troops. One recipe for salt pork, a kind of cured meat similar to bacon, calls for two big pots, each containing 37½ pounds of meat! According to Florence, when mixed with beans, that much salt pork would serve 100 soldiers.

MAKES 2 CUPS

TROPICAL GREEN SMOOTHIE

INGREDIENTS

1 cup stemmed and chopped kale leaves

1 cup frozen pineapple chunks

1 cup frozen mango chunks

1 cup light coconut milk (see the introduction)

Packed with the flavors of pineapple, mango, and coconut, this smoothie tastes like a trip to the beach! Use light coconut milk sold in a can for this smoothie, not the solid kind in a carton in the refrigerated section of the grocery store. You can substitute coconut water for coconut milk.

Place all the ingredients in a **blender**. Place the lid on the blender and hold it in place with a **kitchen towel**. Blend the mixture until smooth, about 1 minute. Stop the blender. Pour the smoothie into a **glass**. Serve.

CARROT CAKE SMOOTHIE

Instead of the Tropical Green Smoothie ingredients, use 1 banana, peeled; 4 ice cubes; 2 carrots, peeled and cut into 1-inch chunks; ¾ cup milk; 1 teaspoon vanilla extract; and ½ teaspoon ground cinnamon. You can substitute any nondairy milk to make this smoothie vegan.

 **FUN FOOD FACT**

Green smoothies were invented by raw foods expert Victoria Boutenko. She had a theory that eating greens in liquid form was the best way to get all their nutrients, but there was a problem: blended-up kale or spinach on its own tasted terrible. So she looked to nature for inspiration. While reading one of primatologist Jane Goodall's books, Victoria came across a story about how chimpanzees would sometimes eat their fruit rolled in leaves. If it worked for the chimps, maybe it could work for humans! Victoria added some bananas to her blended kale, and the refreshing green smoothie as we know it was born.

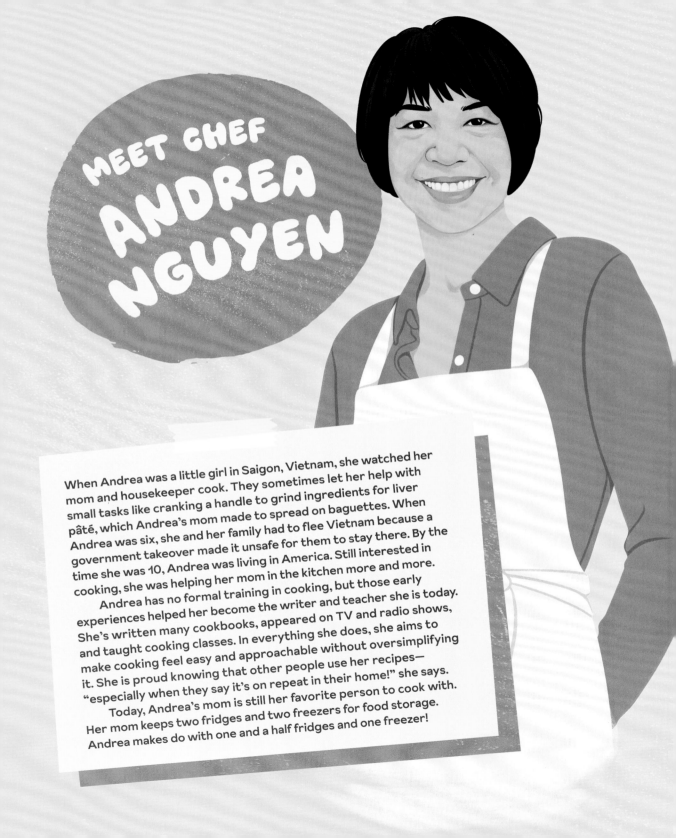

MEET CHEF ANDREA NGUYEN

When Andrea was a little girl in Saigon, Vietnam, she watched her mom and housekeeper cook. They sometimes let her help with small tasks like cranking a handle to grind ingredients for liver pâté, which Andrea's mom made to spread on baguettes. When Andrea was six, she and her family had to flee Vietnam because a government takeover made it unsafe for them to stay there. By the time she was 10, Andrea was living in America. Still interested in cooking, she was helping her mom in the kitchen more and more.

Andrea has no formal training in cooking, but those early experiences helped her become the writer and teacher she is today. She's written many cookbooks, appeared on TV and radio shows, and taught cooking classes. In everything she does, she aims to make cooking feel easy and approachable without oversimplifying it. She is proud knowing that other people use her recipes—"especially when they say it's on repeat in their home!" she says.

Today, Andrea's mom is still her favorite person to cook with. Her mom keeps two fridges and two freezers for food storage. Andrea makes do with one and a half fridges and one freezer!

CHÁO GÀ
OVERNIGHT CHICKEN AND RICE PORRIDGE

SERVES 4

"One of the easiest and most comforting Asian soups is creamy rice porridge. All you do is simmer rice in stock or water. The resulting porridge is called congee in some places, but if you're Vietnamese, you know it as cháo (pronounced like 'chow'). I love to add chicken to make cháo gà, a personal favorite for breakfast (or lunch or dinner). Because simmering can take a good hour and the pot often threatens to boil over, here's my trick: Soak leftover cooked rice overnight (cook while you sleep!), then briefly simmer it the next day to finish. Sauté ground chicken to add to the porridge. Top it with herbs and, if you like, some crunchy fried shallots or fried onions (brands from Thailand and the Netherlands are terrific). That's my easygoing Vietnamese-style chicken and rice porridge." —Andrea Nguyen

1   **For the porridge:** In a **4-quart saucepan**, combine the rice, chicken stock, and water. Cover the saucepan with a **lid** and place in the refrigerator overnight.

2   The next morning, place the ginger on a **cutting board** and use a **chef's knife** to cut it into 3 pieces. Use a **meat mallet** or the bottom of a **heavy mug** to press down on each piece to bruise it. Add the ginger to the pot of rice.

3   Thinly slice the tube-like dark green parts of the scallions and set them aside for the chicken. Add the pale green and white parts to the pot of rice.

4   Set the pot over high heat, cover it partway with the lid (this will prevent the porridge from boiling over), and bring it to a gurgly simmer (small to medium bubbles will appear all over the surface).

5   Reduce the heat to medium-low and simmer, still partially covered, for 15 to 20 minutes, stirring occasionally with a **wooden spoon** or **rubber spatula**. (If the rice starts sticking to the bottom of the pot, lower the heat even more.)

INGREDIENTS

Porridge

2 cups packed cooked long-grain or short-grain white rice (page 176)

5 cups homemade or store-bought chicken stock or broth

2 cups water, plus more as needed

Chubby ¾-inch piece fresh ginger, unpeeled

2 scallions, root ends trimmed

Chicken

1 small yellow onion (about 3 ounces), peeled and thinly sliced (see page 11)

8 ounces ground chicken

1½ tablespoons fish sauce

1 tablespoon canola oil or peanut oil

Fine sea salt

Serving

Recently ground black pepper (optional)

3 tablespoons chopped fresh cilantro or Vietnamese coriander (rau răm—see page 10, optional)

¼ cup homemade or store-bought fried shallots or onions (optional)

CONTINUED

CHÁO GÀ
CONTINUED

6 When most of the liquid has been absorbed (you'll see little separation between the rice and liquid), turn off the stovetop. Use **tongs** to remove and discard the ginger and scallions. Stir the rice, then cover the pot all the way with the lid. Let the porridge rest for 10 minutes.

7 **For the chicken:** While the porridge is cooling, set the sliced onion and scallion greens near the stovetop.

8 In a **medium bowl**, combine the chicken and fish sauce, smooshing them with your (clean) fingers to mix. Wash your hands.

‼ 9 Add the oil to a **10-inch skillet**. Heat the skillet on the stovetop over medium-high heat until the oil is hot but not smoking (see page 17). Add the sliced onion and cook, stirring often with the wooden spoon or rubber spatula, for 3 minutes, or until the onion is fragrant and soft (if you like, cook the onion a little longer, until many pieces are golden and caramelized).

10 Add the chicken, stirring and mashing to break it into small pieces with the wooden spoon or rubber spatula. Keep cooking and stirring for 2 minutes, until the chicken firms up, looks opaque, and isn't pink anymore. Add the scallion greens, stir, and cook until the scallions are softened. Turn off the stovetop.

11 **To serve:** Use a **spoon** or **ladle** to check the thickness of the porridge: It can be rustic and thick, elegant and thin, or somewhere in between—whatever you prefer. If needed, add a splash of water to thin it out or cook the porridge a little longer to thicken it more. Taste and season with up to ½ teaspoon salt (see page 17). Aim for mild saltiness at this point.

12 Bring the porridge to a gentle simmer over medium heat. Taste and season it with more salt by the pinch, if needed. Ladle the porridge into **four soup bowls** and top with the cooked chicken. Garnish with whatever you would like: cilantro, pepper, and/or fried shallots. Eat up immediately.

The smell of rice cooking—whether at her house or wafting from a restaurant kitchen—always reminds Andrea of the coziness of home.

ANY-BERRY MUFFINS

INGREDIENTS

Vegetable oil spray

3 cups all-purpose flour

¾ cup granulated sugar

2 teaspoons baking powder

1 teaspoon table salt

1½ cups milk

⅓ cup vegetable oil

2 large eggs

2 teaspoons vanilla extract

1½ cups blueberries, raspberries, blackberries, chopped strawberries, or a mix

1 tablespoon turbinado sugar (optional)

You can use fresh or frozen berries in this recipe. If using frozen, thaw them and pat them dry with paper towels before stirring them into the batter. An easy way to thaw frozen berries is to spread them out on a paper towel–lined baking sheet and let them sit on the counter for about 20 minutes. If you're using large raspberries or blackberries, cut them in half crosswise. If you're using strawberries, hull them and chop them into ½-inch pieces. Turbinado sugar adds extra crunch and sweetness to the tops of these muffins, but if you don't have it on hand, you can use granulated sugar instead (or skip the sugar sprinkle if you like your muffins less sweet).

1. Set an oven rack in the middle position and heat the oven to 425°F. Spray the inside of each cup of a 12-cup muffin tin and the top of the tin with vegetable oil spray, coating them well.

2. In a large bowl, whisk together the flour, granulated sugar, baking powder, and salt. In a medium bowl, whisk the milk, oil, eggs, and vanilla until well combined.

3. Add the berries to the bowl with the flour mixture and gently stir with a rubber spatula until the berries are coated with flour (this helps keep them from sinking to the bottoms as the muffins bake).

4. Add the milk mixture to the flour mixture and stir gently with the rubber spatula until all the ingredients are just combined and there's no more dry flour (make sure to scrape along the bottom and sides of the bowl as you stir—more dry flour might be hiding there).

5. Use a ⅓-cup dry measuring cup to divide the batter evenly among the greased muffin cups, using the rubber spatula to scrape the batter from the measuring cup. Sprinkle the tops evenly with the turbinado sugar (if using).

6. Place the muffin tin in the oven and bake until the muffins are golden brown and a toothpick inserted into the middle of one of the center muffins comes out clean, 18 to 22 minutes.

!! **7** Use **oven mitts** to remove the muffin tin from the oven and place it on a **cooling rack**. Let the muffins cool in the muffin tin for 15 minutes.

8 Gently wiggle the muffins loose from the muffin tin, then place them directly on the cooling rack (be careful— the muffin tin will still be hot!). Let the muffins cool for at least 10 minutes. Serve warm or at room temperature.

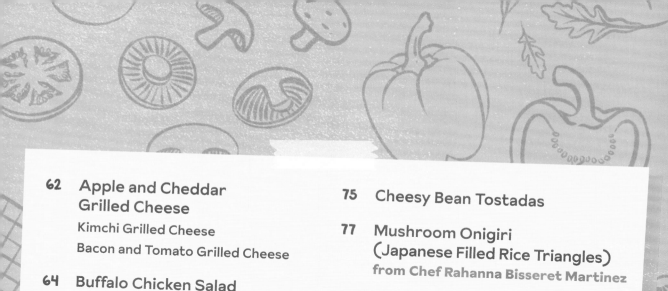

LUNCH

APPLE AND CHEDDAR GRILLED CHEESE

INGREDIENTS

1 tablespoon unsalted butter, softened (see page 17)

2 slices sandwich bread

2 deli slices cheddar cheese, or ½ cup shredded cheddar cheese (see page 16)

3 or 4 apple slices

You can use any melty cheese for this sandwich instead of cheddar: Monterey Jack, pepper Jack, mozzarella, or American cheese all work well. If your bread is on the larger side, you might need to use three deli slices of cheese instead of two (use 1½ slices per layer to cover the surface of the bread). If you'd like to make two sandwiches at once, double all of the ingredients and cook both sandwiches at the same time in a 12-inch nonstick skillet. If you'd like to make a plain grilled cheese sandwich, just skip the apples.

1. Use a **butter knife** to spread half of the butter onto 1 slice of the bread. Place the bread buttered-side down in a **nonstick skillet**.

2. Add 1 slice of cheese (or half of the shredded cheese) on top of the bread. Lay the apple slices on top of the cheese. Top the apple slices with the remaining cheese.

3. Place the remaining slice of bread on top and use your hand to press down gently to stick everything together. Use the butter knife to spread the remaining butter evenly over the top of the bread.

4. Place the skillet on the stovetop over medium-low heat. Cover the skillet with a **lid** and cook until the bottom side of the bread is golden brown (to check: remove the lid, slide a **spatula** underneath the sandwich, and lift it up a little bit to peek underneath), 5 to 9 minutes. If it's ready, slide the spatula under the sandwich, lift it up, and flip it over. Use the spatula to gently press down on the sandwich. Replace the lid and cook until the second side of the sandwich is golden brown, 1 to 2 minutes.

5. Turn off the stovetop. Use **oven mitts** to remove the lid and use the spatula to transfer the sandwich to a **cutting board**. Let the sandwich cool for 2 minutes, then use a **chef's knife** to cut the sandwich in half. Serve warm.

SWITCH THINGS UP!

Kimchi Grilled Cheese

Instead of the apples, use ¼ cup kimchi. Drain the kimchi in a colander or fine-mesh strainer in the sink, pat it dry with paper towels, and chop it with a chef's knife before adding it to the sandwich in step 2.

Bacon and Tomato Grilled Cheese

Instead of the apples, top the sandwich with 2 slices of cooked bacon (see page 51), broken in half, and 1 or 2 slices of tomato in step 2.

📢 FUN FOOD FACT

Former prime minister of New Zealand Jacinda Ardern knows a thing or two about apples: She grew up on an apple farm and was driving a tractor around the orchards even before she learned to drive a car.

BUFFALO CHICKEN SALAD

INGREDIENTS

3 tablespoons mayonnaise

1½ tablespoons mild hot sauce, such as Frank's RedHot Original Sauce (see the introduction)

1½ cups chopped or shredded cooked chicken breast (see page 122)

1 celery stalk, trimmed, cut in half the long way, and sliced thin

1 scallion, trimmed and sliced thin

2 tablespoons crumbled blue cheese (optional)

You can use leftover cooked chicken breast (see page 122) or rotisserie chicken in this recipe. Frank's RedHot Original Sauce is the classic hot sauce for making Buffalo sauce, but other mild vinegar-based hot sauces, such as Texas Pete or Crystal hot sauce, also work. Serve this salad as a sandwich or wrap, or in lettuce cups made from leaves of Bibb or romaine lettuce. To make this vegetarian, swap the chicken for one 15-ounce can of chickpeas, drained, rinsed, and mashed with a potato masher or large fork until about half the chickpeas are broken down.

1. In a **medium bowl**, **whisk** together the mayonnaise and hot sauce.

2. Add the chicken, celery, scallions, and blue cheese (if using). Stir with a **rubber spatula** until all the ingredients are evenly coated. Serve or refrigerate in an airtight container for up to 2 days.

CURRIED CHICKEN SALAD

Instead of the hot sauce, add 1½ teaspoons curry powder and 1 teaspoon lime juice (see page 15) to the mayonnaise in step 1. Instead of the blue cheese, use 2 tablespoons raisins (optional).

 REBEL IN THE KITCHEN

This spicy salad may remind you of Buffalo wings, which some historians believe were invented in 1964 in—you guessed it—Buffalo, New York. One origin story claims that Teressa Bellissimo, who ran a restaurant there, was the first person to cook up the tangy, crispy chicken wings. She paired them with some sides she had on hand: blue cheese and celery.

MEET CHEF LAUREN TOYOTA

Lauren's favorite person to cook with? "Myself. Get out of my way! Haha."

One of Lauren's favorite pastimes as a kid was making a big bowl of boxed mac and cheese and plopping down in front of the TV. Lauren still loves a good mac and cheese, but now she makes her own fully vegan versions. Whenever she tastes those warm gooey noodles, it takes her back to her childhood.

On her website and YouTube channel, and in her two bestselling cookbooks, Lauren cooks up vegan versions of classic recipes. As she puts it, "I make satisfying comfort food that just happens to be made from plants." It took her a while to learn that she didn't have to eat meat and dairy. Now she's excited about teaching her viewers and readers that vegan food can be just as delicious as food made from animal products—if not more so!

If Lauren were hosting a dinner party for Rebels, she'd invite Oprah, Martha Stewart, and Chelsea Handler to gather around her table. She'd serve her own spins on Southern favorites: sautéed greens, biscuits and gravy, mac and cheese, fried "chicken" made from mushrooms, and peach cobbler (all fully vegan, of course).

Lauren is picky about her eggplant. If it's not prepared just right, it's her least favorite veggie, but roasted and served with miso butter or romesco sauce, she finds it "luscious, buttery, and a very interesting vegetable."

CHICKPEA "TUNA" MELTS

"Chickpeas are hearty and perfect to mash up with other tangy, sweet, and crunchy things. You can also fry these sandwiches like a grilled cheese (see page 62)—spread a bit of vegan butter on the outside of the slices of bread before cooking. I find vegan cheese melts best when heated low and slow in a pan covered with a lid to trap in heat. You can also make one sandwich at a time. Refrigerate any leftover chickpea 'tuna salad' and consume it within four days."
—Lauren Toyota

INGREDIENTS

1 (15-ounce) can chickpeas, drained and rinsed

⅓ cup finely chopped celery

⅓ cup finely chopped dill pickles

¼ cup finely chopped red onion (see page 11)

⅓ cup vegan mayonnaise

1 tablespoon lemon juice (see page 15)

1 tablespoon finely chopped fresh dill (see page 10)

1 teaspoon Old Bay Seasoning

¼ teaspoon sea salt

¼ teaspoon pepper

8 slices rye bread

8 slices vegan cheddar cheese

1. Set an oven rack in the middle position and heat the broiler on high.

2. Add the chickpeas to a **large bowl**. Use a **fork** or **potato masher** to mash them until the chickpeas are broken down and mostly smashed. (You still want some texture. They shouldn't be a smooth paste.)

3. Add the celery, pickles, onion, mayonnaise, lemon juice, dill, Old Bay, salt, and pepper. Use a **spoon** to stir until well combined.

4. Place the bread in a single layer on a **rimmed baking sheet**. Top 4 of the slices of bread with the chickpea "tuna salad" and 2 slices of the vegan cheddar cheese each.

5. Place the baking sheet in the oven. Broil until the cheese is melted and the bread is lightly toasted, about 5 minutes. (Watch closely, as your broiling time may vary depending on your oven—you don't want the bread to burn!)

‼ 6. Use **oven mitts** to remove the baking sheet from the oven and place it on the stovetop or a **cooling rack**. Carefully place the 4 plain slices of toasted bread on top of the melted cheese and chickpea "tuna salad." (You could also eat these open-faced without the top slice of bread, if you prefer.) Serve.

FOLDED HAM AND CHEESE QUESADILLA

SERVES 1

Folding your tortilla in fourths makes it easier to add your favorite ingredients without them all falling out. This recipe is loosely based on a Cubano, the iconic sandwich that was first served up in Cuban cafés in Florida.

1 Cut the tortilla and add the mustard, ham, pickles, and cheese as shown in photos 1 and 2 of "How to Fill and Fold Your Quesadilla" (page 72). Shape your folded quesadilla following photos 3 and 4 of "How to Fill and Fold Your Quesadilla."

2 Add the oil to a **10-inch skillet**. Heat the skillet on the stovetop over medium heat until the oil is hot but not smoking (see page 17), about 2 minutes.

3 Reduce the heat to medium-low and use a **spatula** to carefully transfer the quesadilla to the skillet. Cook until the quesadilla is golden brown on the first side, 3 to 4 minutes (to check: slide the spatula underneath the quesadilla and lift up a little bit to peek underneath).

!! 4 When the quesadilla is ready, use the spatula to carefully flip it. Cook until the quesadilla is golden brown on the second side, 1 to 2 minutes. Turn off the stovetop.

5 Carefully transfer the quesadilla to a **plate**. Serve warm.

INGREDIENTS

1 (9- to 10-inch) flour tortilla

2 teaspoons mustard

2 slices deli ham

2 or 3 pickle chips

1 slice deli Swiss cheese

1 teaspoon vegetable oil

📣 FUN FOOD FACT

A traditional quesadilla is made with Oaxaca cheese, which comes from Southern Mexico. According to some historians, Oaxaca cheese was invented by a 14-year-old girl named Leobarda Castellanos García. Leobarda was in charge of making cheese for her family, and she was supposed to check on the milk once it had curdled, or hardened, to the perfect texture. But she accidentally let it sit too long, making a cheese that was crumbly and dry instead. Could she save it? Thinking quickly, she mixed the cheese with hot water, and stringy, stretchy Oaxaca cheese was created.

HOW TO FILL AND FOLD YOUR QUESADILLA

1

Lay the tortilla flat on a cutting board. Use a chef's knife or pizza wheel to cut the tortilla from the center to the edge.

2

Use a butter knife to spread the mustard in a triangle shape on one-quarter of the tortilla, to the right of the cut you just made. Working counterclockwise, place the ham on the next quarter of the tortilla (fold the slices so they fit), followed by the pickle chips on the next quarter, and the cheese slices on the final quarter.

4

Fold the second quarter over the third quarter (with the pickle chips). Finish by folding the remaining quarter (with the cheese) over the third quarter so the folded quesadilla is a triangle shape.

3

Use your hands to fold the first quarter (with the mustard) over the second quarter (with the ham).

CHEESY BEAN TOSTADAS

Tostadas are corn tortillas that have been deep-fried to give them a crunchy texture (kind of like a giant tortilla chip). Look for them at many grocery stores or online. For an even quicker lunch, you can use ½ cup unseasoned canned refried beans—they're already mashed! If you like, add your favorite taco toppings to your tostadas—such as pickled jalapeño slices, thinly sliced radish, chopped cilantro, and/or chopped avocado. If you don't have a toaster oven, make your tostadas in the oven—just heat the oven to 400°F and bake for 4 to 5 minutes in step 4.

1   Set the toaster oven rack in the middle position and heat the toaster oven to 350°F. Line a quarter baking sheet (or the toaster oven tray) with aluminum foil.

2   In a medium bowl, combine the beans, water, cumin, garlic powder, salt, and cayenne pepper (if using). Use a fork to mash the beans until they're mostly broken down and stir in the spices until combined.

3   Place the tostadas on the prepared baking sheet. Use a spoon to spread half of the bean mixture evenly on each tostada, then sprinkle each one with half of the cheese.

4   Place the baking sheet in the toaster oven and bake until the cheese is melted and the beans are warmed through, 5 to 7 minutes.

!! 5   Use oven mitts to remove the baking sheet from the toaster oven and set it on a cooling rack or the stovetop. Use a spatula to transfer the tostadas to a plate. Top each tostada with 2 tablespoons of the salsa and 1 tablespoon of the sour cream. Serve warm.

INGREDIENTS

½ cup black, kidney, or pinto beans, drained and rinsed

1 tablespoon water

¼ teaspoon ground cumin

¼ teaspoon garlic powder

Pinch of table salt

Pinch of cayenne pepper (optional)

2 (6-inch) corn tostadas

¼ cup shredded cheddar cheese (see page 16)

¼ cup salsa

2 tablespoons sour cream

 ## REBEL IN THE KITCHEN

Sabina Bandera is known around the world for her incredible tostadas. She came to Ensenada, Mexico, on her honeymoon when she was 21 and liked it so much that she stayed to open her first food cart and, eventually, a restaurant!

MEET CHEF RAHANNA BISSERET MARTINEZ

Cooking is in Rahanna's genes. Her great-grandmothers Uranie and Fidela were well known in their communities for their kitchen prowess. Every Sunday, Fidela would make tortillas for the entire week—enough to feed the whole family. With 14 kids, that was quite a feat!

If Rahanna were hosting a Rebel dinner party, she'd invite these two incredible women, along with acclaimed author Toni Morrison, who she feels has created a path for her to be a published author. Rahanna says, "I'd love the opportunity to serve women who have given so much to others."

Rahanna published her first cookbook, *Flavor+Us*, in 2023. It's one of her proudest accomplishments as a chef, along with coming in second on *Top Chef Junior* and interning at renowned restaurants like Chez Panisse and Dominique Ansel Bakery. She describes her cooking style as "flavorful food for people who love to cook and care about the planet and people."

Rahanna's favorite kitchen companion? Her eight-year-old brother! She says, "When we cook together from grocery ingredients we both chose, I find he is more open-minded. He is a picky eater, and it's fun to see him change his mind about something he was sure he disliked eating."

MUSHROOM ONIGIRI
JAPANESE FILLED RICE TRIANGLES

"Onigiri are a favorite for my afternoon cravings or meals—they're delicious rice balls with a delightful treasure of fillings inside. You have the freedom to choose from a variety of fillings of your choice. This recipe features a filling crafted from well-seasoned mushrooms, cooked to perfection. I usually have two or three onigiri at a time, so this recipe is great for sharing or you can save the rest of the onigiri in the fridge for later." —Rahanna Bisseret Martinez

INGREDIENTS

1 medium portobello mushroom cap (about 3 ounces)

1 garlic clove, peeled and minced (see page 13)

1 (¼-inch) piece fresh ginger, peeled

1 teaspoon light soy sauce

Pepper

2 teaspoons avocado oil or vegetable oil

1 cup cooked short-grain white rice or sushi rice (page 176)

¼ teaspoon toasted sesame oil

1½ teaspoons toasted sesame seeds

Salt

1 roasted seaweed snack pack

1. Place the mushroom cap on a cutting board. Use a chef's knife to slice it into ¼-inch strips. Slice each strip the short way into ¼-inch pieces. Combine the chopped mushroom and garlic in a medium bowl.

2. Use a rasp grater or the small holes of a box grater to grate your ginger (be careful—stop before your fingers get close to the holes!). Add it to the bowl with the mushroom. Add the soy sauce and a pinch of pepper. Use a spoon to stir until combined. Let sit for 10 minutes.

⚠ 3. Add the avocado oil to a 12-inch skillet or sauté pan. Heat the skillet on the stovetop over medium heat until the oil is hot but not smoking (see page 17). Add the mushroom mixture and cook, stirring occasionally with a wooden spoon or rubber spatula, until the mushrooms have released their liquid, the liquid has evaporated, and the mixture is browned, 10 to 15 minutes. Scrape your cooked mushroom mixture back into the medium bowl and set it to the side for later.

4. In a large bowl, combine the cooked rice, toasted sesame oil, sesame seeds, and a sprinkle of salt. Crumble one seaweed snack into the rice and stir with the wooden spoon or rubber spatula until evenly combined.

CONTINUED

MUSHROOM ONIGIRI
CONTINUED

5   Put on a pair of **disposable gloves**. Measure out ¼ cup of the seasoned rice. Use your hands to roll the rice into a ball and then gently press it into a roughly 3-inch flat disk. (If you don't have gloves, lay a piece of **plastic wrap** on the counter, scoop the rice onto the plastic wrap, and use the plastic to shape the rice.)

6   Add 1 teaspoon of the mushroom mixture to the center of the rice disk. Gently fold up the "sides" of your rice into a ball. Cup your hands together around the ball to form a rice triangle.

7   Use **kitchen scissors** to cut a seaweed snack in half the short way. Wrap one half of the seaweed snack around the edge of the rice triangle—this will give you a nonsticky place to hold your onigiri.

8   Repeat steps 5 through 7 with the remaining filling, rice, and seaweed snacks. Serve. (Wrap any leftover onigiri individually in plastic wrap or place them in a sealed container and store them in the fridge for up to 4 days.)

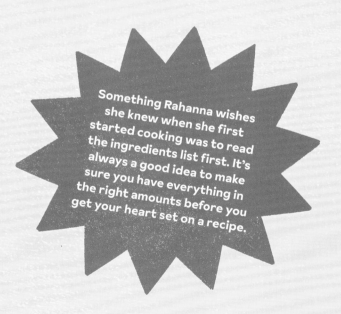

Something Rahanna wishes she knew when she first started cooking was to read the ingredients list first. It's always a good idea to make sure you have everything in the right amounts before you get your heart set on a recipe.

CHICKEN AND VEGGIE BOWL

Bowls are a fun (and delicious!) way to get in touch with your kitchen creativity. Use leftover chicken and rice to make this fresh and yummy bowl. Use what you have on hand in your refrigerator, pantry, freezer, or garden and put your imagination to work pairing different veggies and toppings together.

1 Place the carrot on a cutting board. Using a **vegetable peeler**, peel along the long side of the carrot to make ribbons. Keep going until the carrot is too thin to peel. Set the ribbons aside. Enjoy the rest of the carrot as a snack.

2 In a **medium bowl**, add the rice as your base layer. Add the chicken, carrot ribbons, cucumber, and avocado on top.

3 Use a **spoon** to drizzle the Tahini-Soy Dressing over your bowl. Sprinkle with the sesame seeds and serve.

TEX-MEX SALAD BOWL

Instead of rice, use chopped romaine lettuce as the base. Add ½ cup cooked ground beef, ¼ cup cooked corn kernels, and ¼ cup chopped tomatoes. Drizzle with 2 to 3 tablespoons salsa. Top with as much shredded cheese, chopped cilantro, and pickled radishes as you'd like.

SALMON RICE BOWL

Add ½ cup cooked cubed salmon or tofu and ½ cup cooked baby bok choy on top of the rice. In a small bowl, use a spoon to stir together ¼ cup mayonnaise, ¼ teaspoon sriracha, and 1 tablespoon lemon juice (see page 15) until combined. Drizzle the sriracha mayo onto the bowl. Top with 1 tablespoon each of sesame seeds and sliced scallion.

INGREDIENTS

1 carrot, peeled

1 cup cooked rice (page 176)

1 cooked chicken breast (see page 122), chopped

1 to 2 mini seedless cucumbers, sliced

½ medium avocado, sliced (see page 14)

2 to 3 tablespoons Tahini-Soy Dressing (see page 181)

1 tablespoon sesame seeds

SERVES 2

SUPERFAST, SUPER-EASY CREAMY TOMATO SOUP

INGREDIENTS

1 (14.5-ounce) can crushed tomatoes

½ cup chicken broth or vegetable broth

2 tablespoons heavy cream

1½ teaspoons granulated sugar

¼ teaspoon garlic powder

Salt and pepper

Some brands of crushed tomatoes are chunky and others are smoother. If your tomatoes are chunky but you'd like a smooth soup, at the end of step 3, carefully ladle the soup into a blender, hold the lid down tightly with a folded kitchen towel, and blend until the soup is smooth, about 30 seconds (ask a grown-up for help). If you like, top your tomato soup with chopped fresh basil, Goldfish crackers, croutons, or a dollop of sour cream. If you can't find a 14.5-ounce can of crushed tomatoes, you can use half of a 28-ounce can instead (or double the recipe and use the whole can).

1   In a medium saucepan, use a wooden spoon to stir together the tomatoes and broth. Cook on the stovetop over medium heat until the mixture is simmering (small bubbles appear all over the surface), about 5 minutes.

2   Reduce the heat to medium-low. Add the cream, sugar, garlic powder, ¼ teaspoon salt, and a pinch of pepper and stir until combined. Simmer gently, stirring occasionally, for 5 minutes.

3   Turn off the stovetop. Season the soup with more salt and pepper to taste (see page 17).

4   Use a ladle to transfer the soup to two serving bowls. Serve. (Leftover soup can be refrigerated in an airtight container for up to 2 days.)

 **FUN FOOD FACT**

Cookbook author Eliza Leslie published the first recorded recipe for this kind of tomato soup in 1857, but varieties of tomato soup have existed for even longer than that. There's Spanish gazpacho, which is served cold and was made with other vegetables before colonizers brought tomatoes back to Europe in the 1500s (non-tomato versions are still eaten today). Eastern European borscht, which also dates back to the 1500s, is usually made with beets but can sometimes be made with tomatoes, too.

MEET CHEF ALI SLAGLE

Ali's first memory of being in the kitchen is scooping rice out of the rice cooker with a plastic paddle—there's even a picture of her scooping rice that hangs in her mom's house.

These days, Ali makes food that she describes as "delicious, loving, and realistic." She develops recipes for the *New York Times* and the *Washington Post*, and she's worked as a food stylist and a cookbook editor. She's even published her own cookbook, *I Dream of Dinner (So You Don't Have To)*. Her simple meals are quick and easy to make on busy weeknights—and super delicious to boot.

Something she wishes she knew as a young chef? "You will mess up so much—even when you're an experienced cook."

CAPRESE SANDWICHES ON HOMEMADE FOCACCIA

MAKES 6 SANDWICHES

INGREDIENTS

1 pound pizza dough

3 tablespoons extra-virgin olive oil, plus more for drizzling

Flaky sea salt

2 medium, ripe tomatoes

1 pound fresh mozzarella

3 cups baby arugula

A handful of fresh basil leaves (12 or so)

"When other kids around the lunch table were eating ham and cheese or PB&J sandwiches, I was loving the caprese sandwiches my mom made me for school lunch. With thin slices of juicy tomato and wobbly mozzarella and a tuft of arugula and basil leaves, it is still one of my favorite sandwiches to make and eat. This recipe goes an extra step and makes the bread (using pizza dough!). The bread is crusty and airy like focaccia but a little thinner than usual, so the sandwich has the ideal proportion of bread to fillings. If you don't feel like turning on the oven and baking your own bread, go ahead and use store-bought ciabatta like my mom did for me."
—Ali Slagle

1 About 2 hours before lunchtime, take the pizza dough out of the fridge and let it sit on the counter until it is the same temperature as the room—when you touch it, it shouldn't feel cold at all.

2 Set an oven rack in the middle position and heat the oven to 450°F. Pour the olive oil into a **9-by-13-inch baking pan**. Add the dough and turn to coat it fully in the olive oil. Try not to press it too much or too hard, as that will make for tough bread. Use your hands to press and stretch the dough to fill the pan. If you find that the dough keeps springing back, that means it's still a little cold. Give it a few minutes before trying again.

3 Dimple the top of the dough as if you're playing it like a piano. Take a five-finger pinch of flaky salt and sprinkle it over the dough.

!! 4 Place the baking pan in the oven and bake until the bread is golden on the top and bottom, 15 to 20 minutes. Use **oven mitts** to remove the baking pan from the oven and place it on the stovetop. Carefully use a **spatula** to transfer the focaccia to a **cooling rack**.

CONTINUED

5 While the focaccia is baking, thinly slice the tomatoes and the mozzarella into roughly ¼-inch slices (don't worry too much about getting it exact) on a **cutting board**. Lay the tomatoes out on the cutting board and sprinkle them with a five-finger pinch of flaky salt. (As the tomatoes sit, you'll see they'll release a bunch of liquid. The salt is pushing out the water in the tomatoes so that the tomatoes taste even more delicious in our sandwiches.)

!! 6 When the focaccia is cool enough to handle, use a **bread knife** to cut it into 6 pieces: First, cut it in half the long way. Then, cut each half the short way into 3 equal pieces. Carefully cut each piece horizontally (through the middle) so you have tops and bottoms for your sandwiches.

7 Open up the focaccia so you see the interior cut sides. On the bottom pieces, layer the tomatoes, then the mozzarella, then the arugula and basil leaves. Sprinkle with some flaky salt and drizzle with olive oil, then sandwich with the top pieces of bread. Serve.

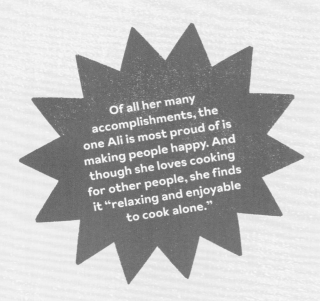

Of all her many accomplishments, the one Ali is most proud of is making people happy. And though she loves cooking for other people, she finds it "relaxing and enjoyable to cook alone."

SNACKS

GUACAMOLE FOR TWO

SERVES 2

In this recipe, the avocado skin works as the bowl for your own personal serving of guacamole. It's a quick and easy way to make a batch of guacamole for two people (and—bonus—there are fewer dishes to wash!). You can also use 1½ teaspoons finely chopped pickled jalapeño slices instead of the fresh jalapeño chile, if you prefer.

1   With each avocado half facing cut-side up, use a **butter knife** to cut 3 lines the long way through the avocado flesh (but not through the avocado skin) and 4 lines the short way (going in the opposite direction) to create a crosshatch pattern.

2   Use a **fork** to gently mash the avocado pieces into chunks inside each avocado skin, scraping along the sides and bottom of the skin but not letting the fork poke through. (Think of the avocado skin as your mixing bowl.)

3   Pour the lime juice evenly over each mashed avocado half. Divide the onion, cilantro, and jalapeño (if using) evenly between the avocado halves. Sprinkle each half evenly with a big pinch of salt. Use the fork to mash and stir the ingredients inside each avocado skin until everything is evenly combined. Serve with tortilla chips.

INGREDIENTS

1 ripe avocado, cut in half and pit removed (see photos 1 and 2, page 14)

Juice of ½ small lime (see page 15)

1 tablespoon finely chopped onion (see page 11, optional)

2 teaspoons chopped fresh cilantro (see page 10, optional)

½ small jalapeño chile, finely chopped (see page 12, optional)

Salt

Tortilla chips, for serving

 REBEL IN THE KITCHEN

It's thought that the Aztecs, indigenous people living in what is now Mexico, invented guacamole. Some historians believe that, at the time, women weren't even allowed to harvest avocados. Luckily that's no longer the case, and tons of female chefs have put their own spin on this creamy dip. Chef, author, and TV host Marcela Valladolid adds mangoes to her guac, while chef and restaurant owner Martha Ortiz garnishes hers with pomegranate seeds.

HUMMUS

MAKES 1½ CUPS

INGREDIENTS

1 (15-ounce) can chickpeas, drained and rinsed

1 garlic clove, peeled and roughly chopped (see page 13)

3 tablespoons tahini

1 tablespoon lemon juice (see page 15)

¼ teaspoon ground cumin

¼ cup extra-virgin olive oil

2 tablespoons water

Salt and pepper

Pita chips, crackers, or cut-up vegetables, for serving

Tahini is a paste made from sesame seeds. Look for it near the peanut butter in your grocery store. Hummus is delicious all on its own, or you can jazz it up with toppings. Spoon the Red Pepper Topping (see opposite) over your hummus, add a sprinkle of za'atar, ground sumac, or paprika, some chopped herbs, or even a dollop of pesto.

1 Transfer the chickpeas to a **food processor**. Add the garlic, tahini, lemon juice, and cumin.

2 Place the lid on the food processor and lock it into place. Pulse until the chickpeas are ground into small pieces, ten to fifteen 1-second pulses.

3 Stop the food processor and remove the lid. Use a **rubber spatula** to scrape down the sides of the bowl.

4 Add the olive oil to the chickpea mixture. Lock the lid back into place and process the mixture for 30 seconds. Stop the food processor and remove the lid. Scrape down the sides of the bowl.

5 Add the water to the chickpea mixture. Lock the lid back into place and process until the mixture is smooth and creamy, about 30 seconds. Stop the food processor.

!!6 Carefully remove the food processor blade. Transfer the hummus to a **small bowl**. Season with salt and pepper to taste (see page 17). Serve with pita chips, crackers, or cut-up vegetables, or store in an airtight container in the refrigerator for up to 5 days.

REBEL IN THE KITCHEN

There are hummus restaurants all over the Middle East, but it's rare for women to own them. Arin Abu-Hamid Kurdi is one of the few female chefs in Israel who runs a hummus shop. One of her specialties is hummus with baharat, a blend of spices that includes cinnamon.

RED PEPPER TOPPING

!! After you've made the hummus, use the rubber spatula to scrape it into a serving bowl. (Make sure to scrape out the processor bowl thoroughly, but you don't need to wash it.) Add ½ red bell pepper, roughly chopped; 1 small garlic clove; 2 tablespoons fresh parsley leaves; 2 tablespoons extra-virgin olive oil; and 1 tablespoon walnuts to the food processor. Lock the lid into place and pulse until the mixture is finely chopped, about ten 1-second pulses. Carefully remove the processor blade. Season with salt and pepper to taste. Spoon the topping onto your hummus and serve.

FRENCH ONION YOGURT DIP

Do you like French onion soup? If you do, you'll *love* this dip! You can serve it with potato chips or pita chips or veggies such as cucumber spears, snap peas, bell pepper strips, or baby carrots. You can double the recipe if you'd like to make lots of dip for a party.

1. In a **medium bowl**, **whisk** together the yogurt, dried onion, mayonnaise, garlic powder, salt, and Worcestershire (if using).

2. Cover the bowl and transfer it to the fridge. Chill until the dried onions soften and the flavors blend, at least 15 minutes.

3. Uncover and sprinkle with the chives (if using). Serve with chips or veggies, or store in an airtight container in the refrigerator for up to 5 days.

INGREDIENTS

1 cup plain whole-milk Greek yogurt

2 tablespoons dried minced onion

1 tablespoon mayonnaise

½ teaspoon garlic powder

½ teaspoon table salt

¼ teaspoon Worcestershire sauce (optional)

1 tablespoon minced fresh chives or scallion greens (optional)

Potato chips, pita chips, or cut-up veggies, for serving

REBEL IN THE KITCHEN

French onion soup was invented in France in the 1600s, but Swiss chef Marie Julie Grandjean Mouquin was the mastermind who made it popular in America in the 1800s. Her version featured rich broth, thick bread, and melty cheese—and was probably served a little hotter than this dip.

MEET CHEF PRIYA KRISHNA

When Priya was very little, her mom would park her on the island in their kitchen while she cooked Indian food. Priya can still remember the smell of cumin seeds toasting in ghee as her mom was swirling them. Her clothes and books were often stained with turmeric.

Today, Priya is a food reporter for the *New York Times* and the author of multiple cookbooks, including *Indian-ish* and *Cooking at Home*. Her newest cookbook, *Priya's Kitchen Adventures*, is for kids. She cooks food that pulls inspiration from around the world, but especially India, where her family is from. She loves to cook dishes that look impressive—and like they took forever to make—but actually come together in a flash.

What is she most proud of? "Trying every day to make how we cook and what we cook more inclusive of all the cultures that call America home."

Priya always thought cooking would be harder to learn because she's left-handed. But that's not true! "Even if you are left-handed, you can still find your way around a kitchen," she says.

MUSHROOM AND CHEESE ROTI PIZZAS

INGREDIENTS

2 tablespoons olive oil, plus extra for drizzling

2 garlic cloves, peeled and minced or crushed (see page 13)

1 small yellow onion, peeled and thinly sliced (see page 11)

12 ounces mixed mushrooms, such as baby bella, shiitake, or oyster, torn into bite-size pieces

½ teaspoon kosher salt

Pepper

¼ teaspoon fresh thyme leaves (optional)

¼ teaspoon red chile flakes (optional)

1 tablespoon lemon juice (see page 15)

4 (7-inch) rotis or (8-inch) whole wheat tortillas

½ cup (4 ounces) crumbled goat cheese or grated Fontina cheese (see page 16)

"This was my mom's solution to my and my sister's pleas whenever we wanted to order pizza for dinner. Rotis are the perfect swap for pizza crust since they crisp up and don't get soggy from all the toppings. This mushroom and cheese variation is great, but feel free to customize it as you like. Look for rotis in Indian or South Asian grocery stores or well-stocked supermarkets. If you can't find any near you, use whole wheat tortillas or any other round bread." —Priya Krishna

1 Set an oven rack in the middle position and heat the oven to 400°F.

2 Add the olive oil to a **large skillet**. Heat the skillet on the stovetop over medium heat until the oil is hot but not smoking (see page 17), about 1 minute. Add the garlic and onion and cook, stirring occasionally with a **wooden spoon**, until the onions turn soft and you can almost see through them, 4 to 6 minutes.

3 Add the mushrooms, salt, a few cranks of pepper, thyme (if using), and red chile flakes (if using). Stir to combine and then cook, stirring only a few times, until the mushrooms turn soft and golden brown on the bottom, about 10 minutes. Turn off the stovetop and stir in the lemon juice.

4 Prick each roti a few times with a fork. (If using tortillas, no need to prick them!) Place them in a single layer on a **perforated pizza pan**, **broiler pan**, or **sheet pan with a wire rack on top**.

5 Drizzle olive oil on each roti (enough to coat the roti but not soak it) and smooth the oil over the surface with your fingers.

!! 6 Place the pan in the oven and bake until the rotis are lightly golden brown, 5 to 7 minutes. Use **oven mitts** to remove the pan from the oven and place it on the stovetop or a **cooling rack**. Keep the oven on.

CONTINUED

MUSHROOM AND CHEESE ROTI PIZZAS
CONTINUED

7 Drizzle each baked roti with a little more olive oil and smooth it over the surface with a **pastry brush** (be careful, the pan will be hot!).

8 Top the rotis evenly with the mushroom mixture and the cheese. Using oven mitts, return the pan to the oven and bake until the goat cheese melts a little (it won't melt completely) or the Fontina is melted and bubbling, 4 to 6 minutes.

!! 9 Remove the pan from the oven and place it on the stovetop or cooling rack. Transfer the pizzas to a **cutting board** and use a **chef's knife** or **pizza wheel** to cut them into quarters. Drizzle with a little more olive oil to finish, then serve.

Priya didn't like cucumbers growing up . . . but then she tried tzatziki, a dip where cucumbers are mixed with yogurt and olive oil and herbs. "It was so creamy and dreamy, it changed my mind!"

**MAKES 5 CUPS
(SERVES 2 OR 3)**

PIZZA POPCORN

INGREDIENTS

1 tablespoon
vegetable oil

¼ cup unpopped
popcorn kernels

2 tablespoons unsalted
butter, melted
(see page 17)

1 teaspoon
tomato paste

½ teaspoon Italian
seasoning

¼ teaspoon table
salt, plus extra for
seasoning

¼ cup grated Parmesan
cheese (see page 16)

Think of popcorn like a blank canvas for flavor: You can use the topping ideas in this recipe, or raid your spice cupboard, refrigerator, or pantry for inspiration. If you like things plain, top your popcorn with 2 tablespoons of melted butter and a sprinkle of salt. You can easily double this recipe if you'd like to make a big bowl of popcorn to share. If you don't have Italian seasoning, you can use ¼ teaspoon dried oregano and ¼ teaspoon dried basil (or ½ teaspoon of either one) instead.

1   In a **large saucepan**, combine the oil and 3 popcorn kernels (these are test kernels that will let you know when the oil is at the right temperature to pop the rest!). Place a lid on the saucepan but leave it slightly ajar, making a small gap but keeping the pot mostly covered.

2   Heat the pot on the stovetop over medium-high heat until the oil is hot and the test kernels pop, 1 to 3 minutes (listen carefully for them to pop, but stand back a bit from the pot in case the oil splashes). Turn off the stovetop and slide the saucepan to a cool burner.

3   Use **oven mitts** to remove the lid. Carefully add the remaining popcorn kernels. Cover the pot with the lid completely and let everything sit for 30 seconds.

4   Return the pot to the warm burner over medium heat. Use oven mitts to set the lid slightly ajar again (this will let steam escape during cooking but keep the popcorn inside the pot). Cook until the popcorn begins to pop vigorously, 1 to 3 minutes.

5   Continue to cook until the popping slows down to about 2 seconds between pops, 1 to 2 minutes longer. Turn off the stovetop and slide the saucepan to a cool burner.

6   Use oven mitts to carefully remove the lid (keep your face away—the steam will be hot!). Transfer the popcorn to a **large bowl**.

CONTINUED

7 In a **small bowl**, **whisk** the melted butter, tomato paste, Italian seasoning, and ¼ teaspoon salt until well combined. Drizzle the melted butter mixture over the popcorn. Use a **rubber spatula** to toss the popcorn until it's evenly coated. Sprinkle the popcorn with the Parmesan cheese and toss again. Taste and season with a little extra salt, if desired (see page 17). Serve.

DILL PICKLE POPCORN

Instead of the tomato paste and Italian seasoning, whisk 1 teaspoon distilled white vinegar, 1 teaspoon dried dill, and ½ teaspoon garlic powder together with the melted butter and salt. Do not use the Parmesan cheese.

FUN FOOD FACT

During World War II, American spies like Virginia Hall undertook dangerous missions to help the war effort. Back at home, people supported the troops in less dangerous ways— by changing their eating habits. The government rationed sugar in order to send it to soldiers overseas. Because of the sugar rationing and the popularity of movie theaters at the time, Americans ate three times more popcorn (a typically salty snack) during World War II than usual.

SPICY HONEY SNACK MIX

SERVES 6 (MAKES 6 CUPS)

A snack mix is easy to customize! Instead of the bagel chips, pretzels, or honey-roasted peanuts called for in this recipe, you can try using other crunchy snacks, like popped popcorn, crushed pita chips or tortilla chips, crackers, or salted mixed nuts. (In this recipe you can also substitute Crispix or Cheerios if you don't have Chex cereal.) Use a mild, vinegar-based hot sauce, like Frank's RedHot Original Sauce, Texas Pete, or Crystal—not a super-hot sauce such as Tabasco.

1 Set an oven rack in the middle position and heat the oven to 250°F. Spray a 9-by-13-inch baking pan with vegetable oil spray.

2 In a large bowl, combine the cereal, bagel chips, pretzels, and nuts. Use a rubber spatula to stir until the snacks are evenly combined.

3 In a small bowl, whisk together the melted butter, honey, hot sauce, sugar, and salt. Drizzle this mixture over the snacks. Stir with the rubber spatula until the snack mixture is evenly coated with the sauce.

4 Use the rubber spatula to transfer the mixture to the greased baking pan and spread it into an even layer.

5 Place the baking pan in the oven. Bake until the mixture is golden brown and crisp, about 45 minutes.

‼ 6 Use oven mitts to remove the baking pan from the oven and place it on the stovetop or a cooling rack. Carefully use the rubber spatula to stir the mixture, scraping up any sauce on the bottom of the pan (the pan will be very hot!). Let the mixture cool completely, about 20 minutes. Serve, or transfer to an airtight container and store at room temperature for up to 1 week.

INGREDIENTS

Vegetable oil spray

3 cups corn, rice, or wheat Chex cereal

1 cup bagel chips

1 cup mini or small square pretzels

1 cup honey-roasted peanuts

4 tablespoons unsalted butter, melted (see page 17)

2 tablespoons honey

1 to 2 tablespoons hot sauce (see introduction)

2 teaspoons granulated sugar

½ teaspoon table salt

FURIKAKE SNACK MIX

Popular in Hawai'i, this snack includes the Japanese condiment furikake, a mix of dried seaweed, sesame seeds, savory flakes made from dried tuna, and salt. Look for it in the East Asian section of your grocery store or online. Instead of the hot sauce, add 2 tablespoons soy sauce to the butter mixture and skip the salt. At the end of step 3, sprinkle the coated snack mix with 2 tablespoons furikake seasoning and stir again until evenly mixed.

FUN FOOD FACT

Young entrepreneur Mikaila Ulmer's interest in honey started with a fear of bees. After being stung as a child, she decided to learn more about bees and discovered how important they are to the environment. Now she makes lemonade sweetened with honey, and some of the proceeds go to help bees all over the world. She's sold more than 2 million bottles so far!

THAI PEANUT-STUFFED CELERY

INGREDIENTS

2 tablespoons creamy or crunchy peanut butter

1 teaspoon lime juice (see page 15)

1 teaspoon toasted sesame oil

1 teaspoon sweet chili sauce

½ teaspoon soy sauce

2 celery stalks, trimmed and cut the short way into 3 pieces each

1 teaspoon toasted sesame seeds or chopped peanuts (optional)

This version of ants on a log—celery sticks filled with peanut butter and topped with raisins—is inspired by peanut-based Thai satay sauce. You can use creamy or crunchy peanut butter in this recipe. Thai-style sweet chili sauce (called nam chim kai in Thai) brings a sweet and tangy punch to the peanut filling and can be found in the East Asian section of most grocery stores. If you don't have it on hand, use ½ teaspoon brown sugar and a dash of hot sauce.

1   In a small bowl, combine the peanut butter, lime juice, toasted sesame oil, sweet chili sauce, and soy sauce. Using a spoon, stir until everything is combined and smooth. (The mixture will look separated at first, but keep on stirring and it will come together.)

2   Use a butter knife to spread the filling inside the celery sticks. Sprinkle them with the sesame seeds or chopped peanuts (if using). Serve.

PIMENTO CHEESE—STUFFED CELERY

Instead of the peanut butter filling ingredients, combine 1 tablespoon softened cream cheese, ½ teaspoon mayonnaise, ⅛ teaspoon Dijon mustard, and a pinch of table salt. Add ¼ cup shredded yellow cheddar cheese and 1 teaspoon jarred diced pimentos that have been drained and patted dry with paper towels. Fill the celery sticks with the cheese mixture, then sprinkle them with sweet or smoked paprika (optional).

 REBEL IN THE KITCHEN

Satay, a type of grilled meat on skewers, is a popular street food in Indonesia and Thailand and is often served with a peanut sauce that inspired the flavors of this recipe. One of the most famous Thai street food chefs is Jay Fai. People wait for hours outside her tiny stall in Bangkok to try her food. She even earned a Michelin star—a huge honor in the culinary world, and exceptionally rare for a street food vendor.

YOU'RE THE CHEF

"I was surprised to really like this! I didn't know what Spam was, so I wasn't sure if I would like it. I really liked the furikake on it."
—Isabelle, age 8

SPAM MUSUBI

This popular Hawaiian snack is made of a block of sushi rice topped with a slice of seared Spam, all wrapped in a piece of nori (dried seaweed). It's similar to Japanese onigiri, balls of rice often filled with different ingredients and wrapped in nori. Make sure the sushi rice and the Spam slices are completely cool before you assemble the musubi in step 7. It's important to use sushi rice in this recipe—its slightly sticky texture helps the musubi hold its shape. Mirin is a type of Japanese rice wine. Look for it in the East Asian section of your grocery store.

1 Add the soy sauce, sugar, and mirin (if using) to a small bowl. Use a spoon to stir until combined.

2 Use a chef's knife to cut the Spam the long way into 6 equal slices. Use kitchen shears to cut each of the nori sheets the long way into 3 equal pieces.

3 Place the Spam slices in a 12-inch nonstick skillet. Use a pastry brush to paint the slices with the soy sauce mixture. Use a spatula to flip the slices over and paint the other side.

4 Place the skillet on the stovetop over medium heat. Cook until the Spam is browned on the first side, 5 to 6 minutes (to check: slide the spatula underneath the Spam and lift up a little bit to peek underneath).

5 Use the spatula to flip the Spam slices and cook until they're browned on the second side, 1 to 2 minutes. Turn off the stovetop.

6 Carefully transfer the cooked Spam to a plate. Let the Spam cool to room temperature, about 15 minutes.

7 Assemble musubi following the photos on pages 110–111 and serve. (The musubi can be wrapped individually in plastic wrap and stored in the refrigerator for up to 3 days.)

INGREDIENTS

2 tablespoons soy sauce

1 tablespoon granulated sugar

1 tablespoon mirin (optional)

1 (12-ounce) can Spam

2 cups cooked sushi rice (page 176)

¾ teaspoon furikake (optional)

2 sheets nori

REBEL IN THE KITCHEN

Versions of Spam musubi were probably eaten in Hawai'i after World War II, but two different women are credited with inventing the dish as we know it today. In the 1980s, Mitsuko Kaneshiro started off making the snack for her kids and was soon selling more than 500 a day out of her shop in Honolulu, Hawai'i. Around the same time, Barbara Funamura was serving it in her restaurant on the Hawaiian island of Kaua'i.

HOW TO SHAPE SPAM MUSUBI

1

Lay a 12-by-10-inch piece of plastic wrap on the counter. Use a ⅓-cup measuring cup to scoop ⅓ cup of rice and place it in the center of the plastic wrap. Use your slightly damp hands to pat the rice into a 4-by-3-inch oval.

2

Sprinkle ⅛ teaspoon furikake (if using) evenly over the rice.

4

Unwrap the musubi and place it back on the plate. Carefully wrap 1 nori strip around the center, tucking the ends underneath. Repeat with remaining rice, Spam, and nori.

3

Place 1 slice of Spam on top of the rice. Gather the edges of the plastic wrap together and twist to enclose the Spam and rice inside. Use your hands to gently press and mold the rice so it matches the shape of the Spam.

MEET CHEF EVA CHIN

Eva's very first memory of being in the kitchen is of stuffing and rolling dumplings with her grandmother. She fell in love with the joyful work of turning raw food into cooked food. As she grew up, food was everywhere. She remembers the smell of satay caramelizing on the charcoal grill in her aunt's courtyard in Singapore. And she treasures the aroma of simmering bone broth wafting through the house. All these experiences helped Eva understand how powerful food can be as a way to celebrate culture and community.

Culture and community play a big part in Eva's work as a chef, and she takes these memories with her wherever she goes. She was the head chef at Avling, a farm-to-table restaurant, and the chef de cuisine at Momofuku Toronto. Now she runs the Soy Luck Club, a supper club that draws on the meals she grew up eating as a kid.

The best part of her job? "I get to make people happy and full," Eva says.

Something Eva wishes she knew when she was first learning to cook: "Seasoning is very important."

PORK AND NAPA CABBAGE DUMPLINGS

"This recipe brings the whole family together. I remember my grandmother kneading the dough while I folded dumplings, my brother chopped ingredients, and my sisters rolled out the wrappers. Cooking together makes memories that will last forever. This recipe is a fun project to tackle with your family and friends. Divide the filling into smaller bowls, give everyone a stack of wrappers, and sit around the table while you fill and shape. If you don't have a food processor, you can finely chop the cabbage and scallions and mince the ginger and garlic by hand. Add them to the large bowl with the pork in step one and continue the recipe with step three." —Eva Chin

1   Place the pork in a **large bowl** and set aside.

!! 2   Add the garlic and ginger to a **food processor** and lock the lid into place. Hold down the pulse button for 1 second, then release. Repeat until the garlic and ginger are minced, 7 to 10 pulses. Remove the lid. Add the cabbage and scallions to the processor bowl. Lock the lid back into place. Pulse until all the ingredients are finely chopped, 8 to 10 pulses. Remove the lid and carefully remove the processor blade.

3   Use a **rubber spatula** to scrape the veggies into the bowl with the pork. Add the wine (if using), soy sauce, salt, pepper, and cornstarch. Stir until all the ingredients are well combined.

4   Cover the bowl with **plastic wrap** and put it in the fridge to marinate for at least 1 hour or up to 3 days before assembling your dumplings.

5   When the filling is ready, fill a **large pot** just over halfway with water. Bring it to a boil on the stovetop over medium-high heat.

CONTINUED

INGREDIENTS

12 ounces ground pork

4 medium garlic cloves, peeled (see page 13)

1 (1-inch) piece fresh ginger, peeled and roughly chopped

1½ cups roughly chopped napa cabbage

4 scallions, trimmed and green parts roughly chopped

¼ cup Chinese cooking wine (optional)

2½ tablespoons soy sauce or tamari

1½ teaspoons kosher salt

1½ teaspoons pepper

1½ tablespoons cornstarch

36 square white wonton wrappers or round white dumpling wrappers

1 tablespoon black vinegar (optional)

1 tablespoon chili crisp (optional)

1 tablespoon chopped fresh cilantro (see page 10) or scallion, for garnish (optional)

PORK AND NAPA CABBAGE DUMPLINGS
CONTINUED

6   While the water comes to a boil, shape your dumplings: Remove the filling from the fridge and discard the plastic wrap. Place a dumpling wrapper on a clean counter and set a **small bowl** of water nearby. Add 2 teaspoons of filling to the center of the wrapper. Use a wet finger to paint the edge of the dumpling wrapper with water. Fold the dumpling wrapper in half over the filling (making a triangle shape if you're using square wrappers or a half-moon shape if you're using circular wrappers). Press the edges tightly together to seal the dumpling and place it on a **tray** or **rimmed baking sheet**. Repeat with the remaining wrappers and filling.

7   Add the black vinegar and/or chili crisp (if using) to the bottom of a **serving bowl** (you can also use any other condiment of your choosing, such as soy sauce or tamari). Set the bowl on the counter near the stove.

‼️ 8   Use a **slotted spoon** to carefully add half the dumplings to the boiling water. Cook, stirring occasionally, until the dumplings float, 3 to 5 minutes.

‼️ 9   Use the slotted spoon to remove the dumplings from the water, draining as much water as possible, and transfer them to the serving bowl. Gently toss the dumplings with the condiments in the bottom of the bowl.

10   Repeat steps 8 and 9 with the remaining dumplings. Garnish with cilantro and/or scallions (if using), or whatever other toppings you might be into. Serve.

The only time Eva enjoyed sweet potatoes was when she had them in Beijing one winter. Street vendors bake frozen potatoes over hot embers, turning them custardy in the center.

SERVES 12

TROPICAL FROZEN YOGURT BARK

INGREDIENTS

2 cups plain whole-milk Greek yogurt

⅓ cup honey

½ teaspoon coconut extract

⅛ teaspoon table salt

1 cup pineapple or mango chunks, patted dry with paper towels

2 tablespoons sweetened shredded coconut

Fresh, canned, or frozen pineapple or mango all work in this recipe. Plan ahead: The bark needs to freeze for at least 4 hours (overnight is even better) before you can break it up and serve it.

1. Line a **9-by-13-inch baking pan** or **small rimmed baking sheet** with **parchment paper**, leaving a little extra hanging over the sides of the pan (this makes it easier to remove the bark later).

2. In a **medium bowl**, **whisk** the yogurt, honey, coconut extract, and salt until well combined and smooth.

3. Use a **rubber spatula** to scrape the yogurt mixture onto the parchment-lined baking pan and smooth it into an even layer. Sprinkle the yogurt evenly with the pineapple and shredded coconut.

4. Cover the pan with **plastic wrap**. Place the pan in the freezer and freeze until solid, at least 4 hours.

5. Remove the pan from the freezer and use the overhanging parchment as handles to lift the frozen bark out of the pan and onto the counter or a **cutting board**. Working quickly (before the bark melts!), use your hands to break the frozen bark into pieces. Serve, or transfer the bark to an airtight container or freezer bag and freeze for up to 1 month.

BERRY FROZEN YOGURT BARK

Use ½ teaspoon vanilla extract instead of the coconut extract. Use 1 cup berries (blueberries, raspberries, blackberries, sliced strawberries, or a mix) instead of the pineapple or mango. If your blackberries or raspberries are large, cut them in half before sprinkling them onto the yogurt mixture. Skip the sweetened shredded coconut.

FUN FOOD FACT

German conservationist Loki Schmidt traveled around the world looking for rare types of plants. On a trip to Mexico in 1985, she discovered a previously unknown kind of pineapple. It was named *Pitcairnia loki-schmidtii* in her honor!

FAiRY BREAD

Fairy bread is a treat traditionally served at birthday parties in Australia, but you can make it for yourself as a snack anytime. Round rainbow nonpareil sprinkles—called "hundreds and thousands" in Australia—are traditional, but if you don't have them, you can use other rainbow sprinkles instead.

1   Use a **butter knife** to spread the bread slice evenly with the butter (make sure to go all the way to the edges of the bread so the sprinkles will stick all over).

2   Pour the sprinkles onto a **rimmed plate** or **shallow dish** and gently shake them into an even layer.

3   Press the bread, buttered-side down, into the sprinkles. Lift up the bread, shake the plate to spread the sprinkles back out, and press the bread down again. Repeat pressing and shaking until all of the empty spots on the buttered bread are evenly covered with sprinkles.

4   Place the bread, sprinkle-side up, on a cutting board. Cut the bread in half diagonally to create two triangles (the traditional shape for Fairy Bread). Serve.

BROODJE HAGELSLAG

In the Netherlands, hagelslag are a type of sprinkles that are often used as a topping for buttered bread. Their name translates to "hailstorm"—perfect for sprinkling! There are lots of flavors of hagelslag, but chocolate is the most popular. Dutch hagelslag have much more cocoa in them than American chocolate sprinkles, and are worth seeking out at a specialty shop or ordering online for extra-chocolaty flavor. To make Dutch broodje hagelslag (sprinkle bread), use hagelslag instead of the nonpareils (in a pinch, you can use American chocolate sprinkles).

INGREDiENTS

1 slice soft white sandwich bread

½ tablespoon unsalted butter, softened (see page 17)

1 tablespoon multicolored nonpareils (round sprinkles)

DINNER & SIDES

OVEN-ROASTED CHICKEN BREASTS

INGREDIENTS

1 tablespoon
kosher salt

1 teaspoon packed
light brown sugar

¼ teaspoon pepper

4 (6- to 8-ounce)
boneless, skinless
chicken breasts

4 teaspoons olive oil

This recipe uses a clever trick to keep roasted chicken breasts moist: starting them in a cold oven. The chicken cooks gradually as the oven slowly heats up, leaving them perfectly juicy by the time they're cooked through. A little bit of sugar on the outside of the chicken breasts helps them to brown in the oven but doesn't make them taste sweet.

1 Set an oven rack in the middle position, but do not turn on the oven. Line a rimmed baking sheet with aluminum foil.

2 In a small bowl, use a spoon to stir together the salt, brown sugar, and pepper.

3 Pat the chicken breasts dry with paper towels. Place the chicken breasts on the foil-lined baking sheet and drizzle each piece with 1 teaspoon of the oil. Use your hands to rub the oil onto both sides of each chicken breast.

4 Sprinkle both sides of each chicken breast evenly with the salt mixture, about ½ teaspoon per side, and rub and pat until evenly distributed. Wash your hands.

5 Place the baking sheet in the cold oven. Heat the oven to 450°F and start your timer. Roast until the chicken is cooked through and beginning to brown underneath, about 30 minutes.

!! 6 Use oven mitts to remove the baking sheet from the oven and place it on the stovetop or a cooling rack. Use an instant-read thermometer to check the temperature of the chicken—make sure the thickest part of each piece reads at least 165°F (see page 17). If the chicken is below 165°F, return it to the oven and roast for 3 to 5 minutes longer, or until it reaches 165°F. Let the chicken breasts cool slightly, about 5 minutes. Serve.

CONTINUED

OVEN-ROASTED CHICKEN BREASTS
CONTINUED

LEMON-PEPPER OVEN-ROASTED CHICKEN BREASTS

In step 2, add 1 teaspoon grated lemon zest (see page 15) to the bowl with the salt and sugar and increase the pepper to ½ teaspoon.

CHILI-LIME OVEN-ROASTED CHICKEN BREASTS

In step 2, add 1 teaspoon grated lime zest (see page 15) and ½ teaspoon mild chili powder to the bowl with the salt, sugar, and pepper.

GARLIC-HERB OVEN-ROASTED CHICKEN BREASTS

In step 2, add 1 teaspoon herbes de Provence or Italian seasoning and ½ teaspoon garlic powder to the bowl with the salt, sugar, and pepper.

SWEET AND SMOKY OVEN-ROASTED CHICKEN BREASTS

In step 2, add ½ teaspoon smoked paprika and ⅛ teaspoon ground cinnamon to the bowl with the salt, sugar, and pepper.

📣 FUN FOOD FACT

In 1923, Cecile Long Steele, who raised chickens for their eggs, ordered 50 chicks. But there was a mistake—500 chicks were delivered! With more birds than she knew what to do with, she started raising them for meat instead. Within three years, she had 10,000 chickens. Cecile is credited with starting the chicken-raising industry in Delaware.

SERVES 4

BROILED CHICKEN "SOUVLAKI"

INGREDIENTS

1 quart (4 cups) cold water, plus extra for soaking skewers

2 tablespoons table salt

2 pounds boneless, skinless chicken breasts

¼ cup extra-virgin olive oil

Grated zest and juice of 1 lemon (see page 15)

1 tablespoon dried oregano

2 garlic cloves, peeled and minced (see page 13)

1 teaspoon honey

½ teaspoon pepper

Vegetable oil spray

Souvlaki are grilled meat and/or vegetable skewers that hail from Greece. To keep these chicken souvlaki as moist as possible, we soak the meat in a mixture of salt and water (called a brine) before cooking. Using the superhot broiler to cook the skewers helps the chicken char and brown, but is much safer and easier than using a grill. Serve your souvlaki with pitas and tzatziki (see page 129) or alongside rice and a salad.

1   In a **large bowl**, **whisk** together the water and the salt until the salt dissolves. (This is your brine—it will help keep the chicken moist and tender during cooking.)

2   On a **cutting board**, use a **chef's knife** to cut each chicken breast the long way into 3 or 4 strips, each about 1½ inches wide. Then cut the strips the short way into about 1½-inch pieces.

3   Add the chicken pieces to the bowl with the brine. Wash your hands. Cover the bowl with **plastic wrap** and put it in the refrigerator. Refrigerate for at least 30 minutes and up to 1 hour. (Don't go longer than 1 hour or the chicken will get too salty.)

4   While the chicken brines, place six **12-inch wooden skewers** in a **baking pan** or **dish** large enough to hold them. Add water until the skewers are covered. Let the skewers soak for at least 15 minutes. (If you have 12-inch metal skewers, you can skip this step.)

5   In a **medium bowl**, whisk together the oil, lemon zest, lemon juice, oregano, garlic, honey, and pepper. (This also is a good time to make your tzatziki sauce [see page 129], if you're making it.)

6   When the chicken is ready, set an oven rack so it is 4 to 6 inches from the broiler heating element and heat the broiler on high. Line a **rimmed baking sheet** with **aluminum foil**. Place a **cooling rack** inside the foil-lined baking sheet and spray it well with vegetable oil spray.

CONTINUED

7 Remove the bowl of chicken and brine from the refrigerator. Line a **large plate** with **paper towels**. Use your hands to remove the chicken from the brine and place it on the paper towel–lined plate. Discard the brine. Pat the chicken dry with extra paper towels.

8 Transfer the chicken to the bowl with the oil-lemon mixture. Use your hands to stir the chicken until the pieces are evenly coated with the sauce.

9 Use your hands to carefully slide the chicken pieces onto the skewers, dividing them evenly and placing the filled skewers on the greased cooling rack set in the foil-lined baking sheet. (Don't pack the pieces of chicken too tightly on the skewers—they should just lightly touch each other. If you have any long and skinny pieces of chicken, fold them in half before adding them to the skewer, which will help them cook more evenly.) Wash your hands.

10 Place the baking sheet in the oven. Broil the chicken pieces until the tops are beginning to char (turn black) in spots, 4 to 7 minutes. (This is a good time to turn on the hood vent over your oven, if you have one.)

!! 11 Use **oven mitts** to carefully remove the baking sheet from the oven and place it on the stovetop or a **second cooling rack** (the baking sheet will be very hot and some liquid will have gathered on the bottom of the pan—don't let it slosh out). Use **tongs** to flip the skewers over.

12 Using oven mitts, return the baking sheet to the oven. Broil until the other side of the chicken is beginning to char, 4 to 7 minutes.

13 Use oven mitts to remove the baking sheet from the oven and place it on the stovetop or cooling rack (the baking sheet will be very hot!). Use an **instant-read thermometer** to check the temperature of the chicken—make sure it reads at least 165°F (see page 17). If the chicken is below 165°F, return it to the oven and broil for 3 to 5 minutes longer, or until it reaches 165°F. Serve.

TZATZIKI

1. Use a **vegetable peeler** to peel the cucumber. Lay a clean **kitchen towel** on a **cutting board** and place a **box grater** on top. Grate the peeled cucumber onto the towel, stopping when your fingers get close to the grater. Discard the cucumber end.

2. Sprinkle the grated cucumber with the salt and let it sit for 10 minutes.

3. While the cucumber sits, in a **medium bowl,** combine the yogurt, oil, vinegar, garlic, pepper, and mint or dill (if using).

4. Wrap the grated cucumber in the towel and hold it over the sink. Twist and squeeze the towel to let as much liquid from the cucumber as possible drain into the sink.

5. Transfer the drained cucumber to the bowl with the yogurt. Stir with a **spoon** until everything is well combined. Taste and season with a little extra salt, if desired (see page 17). Cover the bowl and place it in the refrigerator for at least 10 minutes. Serve. (Tzatziki can be refrigerated in an airtight container for up to 2 days.)

INGREDIENTS

½ English cucumber, or 2 Persian cucumbers

½ teaspoon table salt

1 cup plain whole-milk Greek yogurt

1 tablespoon extra-virgin olive oil

1½ teaspoons red wine vinegar

1 small garlic clove, peeled and minced (see page 13)

¼ teaspoon pepper

2 tablespoons minced fresh mint or dill (see page 10, optional)

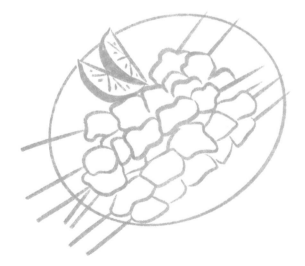

 ## FUN FOOD FACT

People in Greece have been dining on souvlaki since as far back as 2000 BCE! The famous Rebel poet Sappho, who lived around 600 BCE, may have eaten it between composing her odes.

MEET CHEF ANDI OLIVER

Some of Andi's earliest memories revolve around food and family. She remembers preparing weekly Sunday dinners with her mom and dad in Suffolk. When they sat down to eat, it was a time for them to all be together before the busy week ahead.

So it's fitting that Andi describes her cooking today as "food for the family, food for celebration, food to warm the heart and soul." She's run several restaurants and hosted cooking shows, bringing in her love of cuisines from around the world. Growing up, she traveled a lot, and she loved being introduced to new flavors wherever she went. Whenever she eats roti and curry, it reminds her of the first time she went to the Caribbean when she was 16 years old.

Andi's proudest accomplishment is writing her cookbook, *The Pepperpot Diaries*, a celebration of Caribbean food. She wants young chefs to remember that mistakes are important. Her mistakes have helped her better understand the kitchen—and sometimes they're the source of new recipe ideas!

Andi's favorite person to cook with is her best friend, Neneh. They even had their own cooking show together.

Andi thought she didn't like tofu until she tried it in Japanese cuisine. She tasted agedashi tofu, which is deep-fried until it's crispy and golden brown.

HONEY-BAKED CHICKEN WINGS

INGREDIENTS

1 medium onion, peeled and roughly chopped (see page 11)

4 garlic cloves, peeled (see page 13)

1 tablespoon olive oil

Juice of ½ lemon (see page 15)

1 bird's-eye chile, finely chopped (see page 12, optional)

3 tablespoons garam masala

1 tablespoon smoked paprika

A good pinch of salt

2 pounds chicken wings (drumettes and flats)

¾ cup honey

"Everyone in our family loves these honey-baked chicken wings. Eat them when you're happy, eat them when you're sad, just make sure you eat them! Delicious and simple." —Andi Oliver

1. Set an oven rack in the top position and heat the oven to 350°F.

2. Add the onion, garlic, and oil to a **blender**. Put on the lid and hold it in place with a folded **kitchen towel**. Blend until smooth, about 30 seconds. Stop the blender.

3. Pour the onion mixture into a **large bowl**. Add the lemon juice, chile (if using), garam masala, smoked paprika, and salt. Use a **spoon** to stir until well combined.

4. Add the chicken wings to the bowl with the onion mixture and use your hands to toss until they're fully coated. Transfer the chicken wings to a **9-by-13-inch baking dish**, scraping the extra marinade into the dish as well, and spread them into an even layer. Wash your hands.

!! 5. Place the baking dish in the oven and bake for 40 minutes. Use **oven mitts** to remove the baking dish and place it on the stovetop or a **cooling rack**. Use **tongs** to flip the chicken wings over (be careful, the baking dish is hot!). Return the baking dish to the oven and bake for another 30 minutes or until the wings are golden.

6. Use the oven mitts to remove the baking dish from the oven and place it on the stovetop or cooling rack. Drizzle the honey all over the chicken wings. Return the baking dish to the oven and bake until the wings look sticky, about 10 to 15 minutes.

7. Use the oven mitts to remove the baking dish from the oven and place it on the stovetop or cooling rack. Let the wings cool for 5 minutes. Serve with rice and/or salad or eat them all by themselves.

BARBECUE-GLAZED PORK TENDERLOINS

A sweet and tangy DIY barbecue sauce is the perfect glaze for mild pork tenderloins. True barbecued meats are cooked low and slow over burning wood or charcoal, which gives them their signature smoky flavor. This easy recipe uses the oven instead and adds a bit of smoked paprika to the sauce for a hint of smoky flavor—no open fire needed!

1 Set an oven rack in the middle position and heat the oven to 425°F. Line a **rimmed baking sheet** with **aluminum foil**. Place a **cooling rack** inside the foil-lined baking sheet and spray it well with vegetable oil spray.

2 In a **small bowl**, whisk together the ketchup, molasses, vinegar, and smoked paprika. In a **second small bowl**, use a **spoon** to stir together the salt and pepper.

3 Place the pork tenderloins on a large plate. Pat them dry with **paper towels**. Sprinkle them evenly on all sides with the salt and pepper mixture. Transfer the pork to the greased cooling rack set in the foil-lined baking sheet. Wash your hands.

4 Use a **pastry brush** to paint the tops and sides of the pork tenderloins evenly with the sauce.

5 Place the baking sheet in the oven. Roast until the tenderloins are beginning to brown at the edges, 25 to 30 minutes.

‼6 Use **oven mitts** to remove the baking sheet from the oven and place it on the stovetop or a **second cooling rack**. Use an **instant-read thermometer** to check the temperature of the pork—make sure the center reads at least 145°F (see page 17). If the pork is below 145°F, return it to the oven and roast until it reaches 145°F, checking every 3 to 5 minutes.

‼7 Use **tongs** to transfer the pork to a **cutting board**. Let it rest for 5 minutes (this helps the meat hang on to its juices). Use a **chef's knife** to cut the tenderloins the short way into ½-inch-thick slices. Serve.

INGREDIENTS

Vegetable oil spray
¼ cup ketchup
1 teaspoon molasses
1 teaspoon cider vinegar
½ teaspoon smoked paprika
1 teaspoon kosher salt
½ teaspoon pepper
2 pork tenderloins (about 1 pound each)

REBEL IN THE KITCHEN

There are all kinds of barbecue sauces, and every chef makes theirs a little differently. Many serious barbecue cooks—like Helen Turner, who runs Helen's Bar-B-Q in Brownsville, Tennessee—keep their formulas a secret. Customers love Helen's smoky, spicy red sauce, but only she and her staff know the exact ingredients.

SiMPLE SKiLLET CHiLi

iNGREDiENTS

1 (15-ounce) can red kidney, pinto, or black beans

2 tablespoons mild chili powder

2 teaspoons ground cumin

1 teaspoon dried oregano

1 teaspoon brown sugar

¾ teaspoon table salt

½ teaspoon garlic powder

⅛ teaspoon cayenne pepper (optional)

2 tablespoons extra-virgin olive oil

1 onion, peeled and chopped fine (see page 11)

1 bell pepper (any color), stemmed, seeded, and chopped

1 tablespoon tomato paste

1 pound 85% lean ground beef or plant-based ground beef

1 (15-ounce) can tomato sauce or crushed tomatoes

1 tablespoon cornmeal

Be sure to use *chili* powder (a blend of mild chile peppers plus other spices and seasonings) in this recipe, not *chile* powder (just ground chile peppers, which can be quite spicy) for classic chili flavor and mild heat. Top your chili with sliced scallion greens, a dollop of sour cream, shredded cheese, crushed tortilla chips, and/or a squeeze of lime juice. You can serve your chili on its own, alongside a slice of corn bread, or ladled on top of a baked potato, or spooned right into a bag of Fritos to make "Frito pie" (yes, that's a thing!).

1   Set a colander in the sink. Pour the beans into the colander and rinse them with cold water. Let them drain, then shake the colander to release any extra water. Set aside.

2   In a small bowl, use a spoon to stir together the chili powder, cumin, oregano, brown sugar, salt, garlic powder, and cayenne (if using).

!!3   Add the oil to a 12-inch skillet. Heat the skillet on the stovetop over medium heat until the oil is hot but not smoking (see page 17), 2 to 3 minutes. Pick up the handle of the skillet and carefully swirl the oil so it evenly coats the pan. Set the skillet back down on the burner.

4   Add the onion and bell pepper and cook, stirring occasionally with a wooden spoon, until the vegetables have softened, about 5 minutes.

5   Stir in the spice mixture and the tomato paste and cook until the mixture smells fragrant and the tomato paste darkens, about 1 minute.

6   Carefully add the ground beef. Cook, breaking up the meat into small pieces with the wooden spoon, until the meat is no longer pink, about 5 minutes.

7   Stir in the tomato sauce and the drained beans. Use the wooden spoon to scrape up any browned bits on the bottom

CONTINUED

of the skillet. Fill the empty tomato sauce can with water and pour that into the skillet (the skillet will be very full). Bring the mixture to a simmer (small bubbles appear all over the surface), about 5 minutes.

8 Turn down the heat to medium-low and simmer, stirring occasionally, until the chili has slightly thickened, about 10 minutes.

9 Stir in the cornmeal and cook, stirring occasionally, until the chili is thick, 10 to 15 minutes longer. Turn off the stovetop. Let the chili sit for 5 minutes, then taste and season with a little extra salt, if desired (see page 17). Ladle the chili into bowls and serve.

FUN FOOD FACT

In San Antonio, Texas, in the 1880s, food stands began popping up in open-air plazas. At each stall, women sold foods such as tamales, enchiladas, and chili con carne. These cooks were known as Chili Queens, and they were responsible for popularizing many delicious Mexican dishes in the United States.

CRISPY SHEET PAN GNOCCHI WITH SAUSAGE AND BROCCOLI

INGREDIENTS

2 garlic cloves, peeled and minced (see page 13)

½ teaspoon table salt

¼ teaspoon black pepper

½ teaspoon crushed red pepper flakes (optional)

2 tablespoons plus 2 tablespoons extra-virgin olive oil, measured separately, plus extra for drizzling

5 cups broccoli florets, large florets cut in half (about 12 ounces)

1 pound shelf-stable potato gnocchi

1 pound loose sweet or hot Italian sausage meat

Juice of ½ lemon (see page 15)

¼ cup grated Parmesan cheese (see page 16, optional)

Gnocchi are a type of Italian dumplings made with mashed potatoes. When boiled, they become soft and chewy throughout, but when they're baked, they become crispy on the outside and tender on the inside. For this recipe, look for potato gnocchi sold in vacuum-sealed, shelf-stable packages, usually near the pasta or in the Italian section of your grocery store. If you can't find loose Italian sausage meat, you can use 1 pound of Italian sausage links instead. Use kitchen shears to snip through the casing of each sausage the long way, then peel off and discard the casings.

1   Set an oven rack in the lower-middle position and heat the oven to 450°F. Line a rimmed baking sheet with parchment paper.

2   In a large bowl, whisk together the garlic, salt, black pepper, red pepper flakes (if using), and 2 tablespoons of the oil. Add the broccoli and use a rubber spatula to stir until it's evenly coated with oil.

3   Transfer the broccoli to the center of the parchment-lined baking sheet and spread it into an even layer, leaving empty space around the edges.

4   Add the remaining 2 tablespoons oil to the now-empty bowl, then add the gnocchi, using your hands to separate any pieces that are stuck together. Stir with the rubber spatula until the gnocchi are evenly coated with oil.

5   Transfer the gnocchi to the empty edges of the baking sheet around the broccoli, pushing them up against the rim of the pan (this helps them get extra crispy).

6   Use a spoon or your fingers to drop dollops of the sausage meat all over the baking sheet on top of the gnocchi and vegetables.

CONTINUED

7 Place the baking sheet in the oven. Bake until the sausage and broccoli are browned and the gnocchi is becoming crispy on the bottom, 20 to 25 minutes.

!!8 Use **oven mitts** to remove the baking sheet from the oven and place it on the stovetop or a **cooling rack**. Let cool slightly, about 3 minutes.

9 Use a **spatula** to divide the gnocchi, broccoli, and sausage evenly among serving bowls (be careful—the baking sheet will be hot). Drizzle each bowl evenly with the lemon juice and a little extra oil, then top with a sprinkle of the Parmesan cheese (if using). Serve.

YOU'RE THE CHEF
"I liked how the gnocchi was a bit crispy on the outside and chewy on the inside."
–Arden, age 9

PICADILLO
GROUND BEEF WITH TOMATOES AND OLIVES

INGREDIENTS

2 chayote squash, chopped, or 8 ounces small potatoes, cut into quarters (or ½-inch pieces if on the bigger side)

1 medium tomato (6 ounces), cut into quarters

1 cup fresh cilantro leaves and stems, roughly chopped, plus ¼ cup cilantro leaves for serving, measured separately (see page 10)

1 small onion, peeled and quartered (see page 11)

3 garlic cloves, peeled (see page 13)

2 tablespoons extra-virgin olive oil

1 pound 90% lean ground beef

2½ teaspoons sazón (see the introduction)

2 teaspoons distilled white vinegar

½ cup chicken broth

2 tablespoons pitted manzanilla olives (optional)

Salt and pepper

Picadillo is a ground beef dish, often combined with tomatoes and olives. You'll find lots of variations all over Latin America and the Caribbean. This version uses chayote, a small green squash native to Mexico—look for it in the produce section of your grocery store or in Asian or Caribbean markets. If you prefer potatoes instead, use ones labeled "baby" or "new." Sazón is a spice mix popular across Latin America (look for it in the spice aisle of your grocery store, in Latin American markets, or online). To make this recipe vegan, use plant-based beef and vegetable broth. Serve your picadillo over white rice (page 176) and with Oven-Roasted Maduros (page 191) on the side.

!!1 Place the chayote on a **cutting board**. Use a **chef's knife** to slice around the core, cutting the chayote into 4 large pieces. Discard the core. Place the pieces flat-side down on the cutting board. Slice them the long way into ½-inch-wide strips. Rotate the strips and slice them the short way into ½-inch pieces. Set aside.

2 Add the tomato, cilantro, onion, and garlic to a **food processor** and lock the lid into place. Hold down the pulse button for 1 second, then release. Repeat until the vegetables are coarsely chopped, 12 to 14 pulses. Remove the lid and carefully remove the processor blade.

!!3 Add the oil to a **12-inch skillet**. Heat the skillet on the stovetop over medium-high heat until the oil is hot but not smoking (see page 17), about 2 minutes. Pick up the handle of the skillet and carefully swirl the oil so it evenly coats the pan. Set the skillet back down on the stovetop.

4 Add the ground beef to the skillet and cook, breaking up the meat into small pieces with a **wooden spoon**, until it's no longer pink and begins to brown, about 5 minutes.

5 Add the sazón and vinegar and stir to combine. Cook for 1 minute. Turn down the heat to medium.

6 Add the chopped tomato mixture and cook, stirring occasionally, until simmering, 3 to 4 minutes.

7 Add the broth, chayote, and olives (if using) and stir until well combined. Cook, stirring occasionally, until the chayote is tender when poked with a fork and the liquid has mostly evaporated, 20 to 25 minutes. Turn off the stovetop.

8 Season with salt and pepper to taste (see page 17). Sprinkle the picadillo with the remaining cilantro. Serve.

YOU'RE THE CHEF

"It was delicious and flavorful, with a perfect texture. I highly enjoyed it, and it's a great family meal."
—Goldie, age 11

KOFTE
MIDDLE EASTERN MEATBALLS

INGREDIENTS

½ onion, peeled and cut into quarters (see page 11)

1 garlic clove, peeled (see page 13)

½ cup fresh parsley leaves and stems, roughly chopped (see page 10)

1 pound 85% lean ground beef or ground lamb

1 teaspoon ground cumin

¾ teaspoon table salt

¼ teaspoon ground cinnamon

¼ teaspoon ground allspice

¼ teaspoon pepper

Kofte, kebabs made of ground meat, are popular throughout the Middle East as well as in Turkey and Armenia. They're often flavored with spices and herbs and cooked on a grill. To make things a little easier and safer, we took this version off of the skewer and baked the kofte in the oven. If you don't have a food processor, you can use a chef's knife to finely chop the onion, garlic, and parsley and mix them together in a large bowl. Serve your kofte with flatbreads (page 182), rice (page 176), a salad, and/or roasted vegetables (page 178).

1   Set an oven rack in the middle position and heat the oven to 425°F. Line a **rimmed baking sheet** with **parchment paper**.

2   Add the onion, garlic, and parsley to a **food processor**. Lock the lid into place. Hold down the pulse button for 1 second, then release. Repeat until the vegetables are finely chopped, about ten 1-second pulses.

!!3   Remove the lid and carefully remove the processor blade. Use a **rubber spatula** to scrape the onion mixture into a **large bowl**.

4   Add the beef, cumin, salt, cinnamon, allspice, and pepper to the now-empty food processor bowl. Lock the lid into place. Pulse until the ingredients are well combined, ten to fifteen 1-second pulses.

!!5   Remove the lid and carefully remove the processor blade. Use the rubber spatula to transfer the meat mixture to the large bowl with the onion mixture. Stir until well combined.

6   Use lightly wet hands to divide the meat mixture into 10 equal portions. Shape each portion into an oval that's about 3½ inches long and 1¼ inches thick. As you finish forming each kofte, place it on the parchment-lined baking sheet, leaving space between them.

7   Place the baking sheet in the oven. Bake until the kofte are cooked through and golden brown, 12 to 15 minutes.

!!**8** Use **oven mitts** to remove the baking sheet from the oven and place it on the stovetop or a **cooling rack**. Use an **instant-read thermometer** to check the temperature of the kofte—make sure it reads at least 160°F (see page 17). If the kofte are below 160°F, return the baking sheet to the oven and bake for 3 to 5 minutes longer, or until the kofte reach 160°F. Let the kofte cool slightly, 2 to 3 minutes. Serve.

YOU'RE THE CHEF

"The kofte offers a lot of flavor with its perfectly seasoned meat, making it tasty and fun to cook. The texture was really soft and super flavorful. The ingredients and method of cooking them made the recipe delicious and thoughtfully created." –Ariana, age 10

FISH STICK TACOS WITH CREAMY HONEY-LIME SLAW

INGREDIENTS

1 tablespoon extra-virgin olive oil

1 teaspoon Old Bay Seasoning

16 to 18 frozen fish sticks

2 tablespoons sour cream

2 tablespoons mayonnaise

Zest and juice of 1 lime (see page 15)

1 teaspoon honey

¼ teaspoon table salt

4 cups shredded coleslaw mix

2 tablespoons chopped fresh cilantro (see page 10, optional)

8 to 10 (6-inch) corn tortillas

A classic fish taco is made with deep-fried fish, but this quick and easy version uses fish sticks instead. They bake up crispy on the outside and tender on the inside and nestle perfectly into corn tortillas. Try jazzing up your tacos with extra toppings, such as pickled onions or jalapeño chiles, a drizzle of Mexican crema, a dash of hot sauce, sliced radishes, diced avocado, and/or extra chopped cilantro.

1   Set an oven rack in the middle position and heat the oven to 425°F. Line a **rimmed baking sheet** with **parchment paper**.

2   In a **large bowl**, use a **rubber spatula** to stir together the oil and Old Bay. Add the frozen fish sticks and stir until they are evenly coated.

3   Transfer the fish sticks to the parchment-lined baking sheet and spread them into an even layer.

4   Place the baking sheet in the oven. Bake until the fish sticks are cooked through and deep golden brown, 16 to 20 minutes.

5   While the fish sticks bake, in a **second large bowl**, **whisk** together the sour cream, mayonnaise, lime zest, lime juice, honey, and salt. Add the coleslaw mix and cilantro (if using) and use **tongs** to toss until well combined.

!! 6   When the fish sticks are ready, use **oven mitts** to remove the baking sheet from the oven and place it on the stovetop or a **cooling rack**. Let the fish sticks cool on the baking sheet for 5 minutes.

7   Meanwhile, stack the tortillas on a **small microwave-safe plate** and cover them with a **damp dish towel**. Heat the tortillas in the microwave until warm, about 1 minute.

8   Use the tongs to divide the fish sticks among the warmed tortillas. Top the fish sticks with the slaw and serve with your favorite taco toppings (see the introduction), if desired.

MEET CHEF ASMA KHAN

When Asma thinks about her childhood kitchen in Calcutta, India, she remembers Bollywood music playing from the battery-powered radio, which came in handy when there were power outages. She remembers watching her mom make parathas, a type of flatbread, on a tawa, a flat iron griddle. One day, as Asma was eating a paratha on the balcony, a crow came by and stole it from her!

Every day, she would wake up to the sound of roasted spices being crushed with a traditional stone mortar and pestle. Her mom had a catering business, and all the spices were freshly roasted and ground in the mornings. Even without looking at the clock, Asma knew what time it was from the sound of the spice preparation.

Asma's recollections of home and childhood are present in everything she cooks. As she puts it, "The food I make is not just a recipe, it is infused with my heritage and memories." At her restaurant in London, the Darjeeling Express, her all-women team serves up Indian food from across the country. The restaurant opened in 2017, and despite challenges and closures during the COVID-19 pandemic, the core kitchen team has stayed the same. Asma thinks the true sign of a good chef is being a team player and holding the kitchen together on good days as well as bad days.

Asma's best cooking advice: Don't panic! When she was starting out, she was afraid to use hot oil, frightened it would splash her when she dropped food in. Eventually, she learned to slide food in from the side, which is much safer.

SALMON KABAB PATTIES

INGREDIENTS

1½ pounds small red or yellow potatoes

15 ounces canned boneless cooked salmon or tuna, drained

Vegetable oil

½ medium yellow onion, peeled and chopped (see page 11)

½ teaspoon ground turmeric

¼ teaspoon cayenne pepper or paprika

1 large egg

2 tablespoons chopped fresh cilantro leaves (see page 10)

2 tablespoons panko bread crumbs, plus more if needed

¾ teaspoon table salt

"This dish is so evocative of Calcutta, the city in India where I grew up. My parents would often prepare these patties when unexpected guests turned up at our home, and usually served them with a simple accompaniment of rice and dal. But I loved to eat my kabab with ketchup and buttered toast! This is still my go-to recipe when I have to prepare something in a hurry, as it can be made with common cupboard ingredients and potatoes." —Asma Khan

1   Add the potatoes to a large saucepan. Add water to the saucepan until it covers the potatoes by about 1 inch. Bring the water to a boil over medium-high heat. Cook until the potatoes are soft enough to easily pierce with a fork, 20 to 30 minutes.

‼ 2   Set a colander in the sink. Ask a grown-up to drain the potatoes in the colander. Let the potatoes cool until they are not too hot to touch, then get an adult to help you remove their skins. Transfer the potatoes to a large bowl. Use a potato masher to mash the potatoes until they're mostly smooth.

3   Add the salmon to the bowl with the mashed potatoes and use a wooden spoon to stir until combined.

4   Add 4 tablespoons oil to a 12-inch nonstick skillet. Heat the skillet on the stovetop over medium heat until the oil is hot but not smoking (see page 17), about 2 minutes. Add the onion and cook, stirring occasionally with the wooden spoon, until the onion is golden brown, 5 to 7 minutes.

5   Add the turmeric and cayenne and cook, stirring constantly, for 30 seconds. Turn off the stovetop. Scrape the onion mixture into the bowl with the salmon and potatoes and stir until well combined.

6   Add the egg, cilantro, bread crumbs, and salt to the bowl. Use the wooden spoon to stir until well combined. The mixture should be firm (if it seems too wet, add more bread crumbs, a little at a time, until it's firm).

CONTINUED

SALMON KABAB PATTIES
CONTINUED

7   Use your hands to shape the salmon mixture into 16 little circles, about 2 inches wide and about ½ inch high (about ¼ cup per patty). As you form each patty, place it on a **rimmed baking sheet**. Wash your hands.

8   Wipe out the 12-inch nonstick skillet with **paper towels**. Add 2 tablespoons oil to the skillet. Heat the skillet on the stovetop over medium heat until the oil is hot but not smoking, about 2 minutes. Carefully add half the patties to the skillet and cook until they're golden brown on the first side, 2 to 3 minutes (to check: use a **spatula** to lift up one patty and peek underneath).

9   Use the spatula to flip the patties and cook until they're golden brown on the second side, 2 to 3 minutes. Transfer the patties to a **serving platter** or **plate**. Repeat to cook the remaining patties. Serve with a tomato-based dip or any other dip of your choice.

Asma's favorite person to cook with is her son, Aziz. She hopes he will become the custodian of her family recipes.

PASTA WITH MARCELLA HAZAN'S TOMATO SAUCE

Since there are so few ingredients in this recipe, high-quality canned tomatoes are key for the best flavor and texture. San Marzanos are prized in Italy for their flavor, so look for imported Italian brands of canned San Marzano tomatoes, such as Gustarosso, Alessi, Bianco DiNapoli, Pastene, or Cento. The American brands San Merican and Muir Glen use tomatoes similar to San Marzanos and are also good options for this recipe.

1   **For the sauce:** In a large saucepan, combine the tomatoes and their juices, the onion halves, the butter, and the salt.

2   Place the saucepan on the stovetop over medium heat. Cook, stirring occasionally with a wooden spoon, until the butter melts and the mixture comes to a simmer (small bubbles appear all over the surface), 6 to 8 minutes.

3   Spoon out a little bit of the sauce into a small bowl and let it cool slightly. Taste the sauce. If you'd like it to be sweeter, add the optional sugar to the pot, ½ teaspoon at a time, tasting in between additions to see how you like the flavor. (The sugar won't make your sauce taste sweet. It's there to balance out the acidity of the tomatoes.)

4   Reduce the heat to medium-low. Gently simmer the sauce, stirring occasionally and carefully breaking open and mashing the tomatoes with the spoon, until the tomatoes have softened and the sauce has thickened, about 45 minutes.

5   **For the pasta:** Meanwhile, add the water to a large pot. Place the pot on the stovetop and bring the water to a boil over high heat.

6   Add the salt to the water, then carefully add the pasta. Cook, stirring occasionally with a clean wooden spoon, until the pasta reaches the cooking time listed on the package for al dente pasta. Turn off the stovetop.

CONTINUED

INGREDIENTS

Tomato Sauce

1 (28-ounce) can whole peeled tomatoes (see the introduction), with their juices

1 medium onion, halved through the root end and peeled (see page 11)

5 tablespoons unsalted butter, cut into 8 pieces

⅛ teaspoon table salt

½ to 1 teaspoon granulated sugar (optional)

Pasta

4 quarts water

1 tablespoon table salt

1 pound pasta (any shape will do)

1 tablespoon extra-virgin olive oil

Grated Parmesan cheese (see page 16, optional)

Chopped fresh basil or parsley (see page 10, optional)

!!7 Set a colander in the sink. Ask a grown-up to drain the pasta in the colander.

8 Add the oil to the now-empty pot. Add the drained pasta and stir with the wooden spoon until the pasta is coated with oil. (If you're using a long pasta shape, like spaghetti, it's easier to do this with a pair of tongs.) Put a lid on the pot to keep the pasta warm.

9 When the sauce is ready, turn off the stovetop and slide the saucepan to a cool burner. Use tongs to remove the onion halves (you can discard them or let them cool and eat them as a chef's snack). Use a potato masher to carefully mash any remaining large tomato pieces until they're broken down (be careful—the sauce and the saucepan will be hot, so look out for splashes!). Taste the sauce and season with a little more salt, if desired (see page 17).

10 Use the tongs (for long noodles) or a large spoon (for short pasta shapes) to portion the warm pasta among serving bowls. Spoon the sauce over the pasta, dividing it evenly. Sprinkle each portion with some grated Parmesan cheese and/or basil (if using). Buon appetito!

FUN FOOD FACT

Marcella Hazan was a pioneering writer and cooking instructor who taught Americans all about authentic Italian cuisine through her classes and cookbooks starting in the 1960s. This recipe is one of her most famous, probably because it is so simple yet so delicious.

BASIL PESTO

Pick the basil leaves from the stems and pack them tightly into a dry measuring cup to measure 2 cups of leaves. To make this recipe vegan, skip the Parmesan cheese and increase the nuts to ½ cup. For a nut-free pesto, you can use sunflower seeds or pepitas instead of the nuts. You can serve this pesto over cooked pasta (see steps 5 to 7, pages 153–154), spread onto a sandwich, or dolloped onto cooked chicken (page 122), fish, or roasted vegetables (page 178).

INGREDIENTS

2 cups fresh basil leaves

¼ cup pine nuts, walnuts, or almonds

1 garlic clove, peeled and roughly chopped (see page 13)

¼ teaspoon table salt

½ cup extra-virgin olive oil

¼ cup grated Parmesan cheese (see page 16)

1 Add the basil, pine nuts, garlic, and salt to a **food processor**. Lock the lid into place. Hold down the pulse button for 1 second, then release. Repeat until everything is finely chopped, about twelve 1-second pulses.

2 Remove the lid and use a **rubber spatula** to scrape down the sides of the bowl. Lock the lid back into place.

3 Turn on the processor. With the processor running, slowly pour the oil into the processor through the feed tube. Process until a smooth sauce forms, about 30 seconds. Stop the processor.

!!4 Remove the lid and carefully remove the processor blade. Use the rubber spatula to scrape the pesto into a **small bowl**. Stir in the Parmesan cheese. Taste and season with a little extra salt, if desired (see page 17). Serve, or transfer to an airtight container, drizzle some extra oil on top (this helps keep the pesto from turning brown), and refrigerate for up to 4 days.

PLAY WITH YOUR PESTO

For a twist on classic basil pesto, swap out half of the basil in this recipe for another green ingredient. Try using 1 cup parsley, baby kale, baby spinach, or baby arugula plus 1 cup basil. You can even make pesto from vegetable tops that might otherwise go in the compost. Try using 1 cup feathery carrot tops, peppery radish tops, or hardy beet greens for an extra flavor boost and to reduce food waste.

FUN FOOD FACT

Basil pesto originated in the Liguria region of Italy in the 1800s. Liguria was also home to Rebels like Maria Pellegrina Amoretti, the first woman ever to graduate with a law degree from an Italian university, and Irene Brin, a fashion journalist who spoke out against the Nazis during World War II.

MEET CHEF HETTY LUI MCKINNON

As a kid, whenever Hetty was feeling sick, her mom would make ginger fried rice. From her bed, Hetty would hear the spatula scraping against the wok, and soon, the comforting aroma of ginger would fill the house. It was her mom's special recipe for times when the body needs to heal and recover. She even brought it to the hospital after Hetty had her first baby.

Hetty's usually the boss in the kitchen, but when she cooks with her mom, even today, she becomes the sous chef. She loves listening to her mom's advice and stories about her life in China before she moved to Australia.

As a food writer and cookbook author, Hetty focuses on vegetarian comfort food. She describes her recipes as "a celebration of my Chinese heritage, mixing in global influences from growing up in Australia and living in the world." She feels strongly about giving a voice to children of immigrants, like her, who often have a hard time finding a sense of belonging. Food, she believes, is a great way to build bridges and community, to help people from different backgrounds find things in common. Most of all, she loves that her recipes make cooking easier and more delicious for people around the world.

Hetty's best cooking advice: "Use all your senses in the kitchen. Learn to listen to the pop of the rice to know when it's ready, to smell the pan-fried noodles to know when they are perfectly crispy, to look at the color of pastry to know when it's ready. Cooking is a multi-sensory experience, and when we learn to trust our senses, we will be better cooks."

SHEET PAN VEGETABLE CHOW MEIN WITH TOFU

SERVES 4

"This chow mein recipe is inspired by my mother's colorful and textural Cantonese chow mein. While the term 'chow mein,' which translates to 'fry noodles,' has come to represent a variety of stir-fried noodle dishes at Chinese American restaurants, the Cantonese and Hong Kong version is very specific. The noodles should be crispy on the bottom but soft on the top, covered with lightly sauced crisp-tender vegetables (and meat or seafood). While a wok is still the best way to make chow mein, I have devised my own cooking technique using a sheet pan and high oven heat that gives me similar textures and flavors to my mother's dish, while being less hands-on. Traditional chow mein is made using egg noodles because they get really crispy, but here, I've opted for dried instant ramen noodles, which work just as well.

"One of the best things about this dish is that it is very adaptable. Feel free to replace the vegetables with whatever you have in the fridge. Carrots, cauliflower, asparagus, snow peas, cabbage, or zucchini would all be excellent substitutes or additions."
—Hetty Lui McKinnon

1   **For the noodles and vegetables:** Set oven racks in the middle and bottom positions and heat the oven to 425°F.

2   Pat the tofu dry with a clean kitchen towel. Place the tofu on a cutting board. Use a chef's knife to slice it the short way into ¼-inch-thick pieces. Lay each piece flat-side down and slice it in half the long way (so you get two long strips). Place the tofu strips into a shallow bowl and pour over the sesame oil and soy sauce. Gently turn the tofu in the oil and sauce until the strips are well coated. Set aside to marinate for 5 minutes.

3   You will need two rimmed baking sheets: On the first baking sheet, lay out the tofu slices. On the second baking sheet, add the broccoli, shiitake mushrooms, and bell pepper. Drizzle the vegetables with 1 tablespoon of the neutral oil and sprinkle with 1 teaspoon salt and a big pinch of black or white pepper. Use your hands to toss the vegetables to coat them with the oil and seasoning.

INGREDIENTS

Noodles and Vegetables

1 block extra-firm tofu, drained

1 tablespoon sesame oil (toasted or untoasted)

1 tablespoon soy sauce or tamari

1 head broccoli (14 ounces), cut into small florets

4 ounces shiitake mushrooms, stems trimmed and discarded, caps sliced

1 red or green bell pepper, thinly sliced

1 tablespoon plus 1 to 2 tablespoons neutral oil, such as vegetable or canola, measured separately

Kosher salt and black or white pepper

3 packages instant ramen noodles (about 9 ounces total, if there are flavor packets, discard them)

Boiling water, for the noodles

CONTINUED

SHEET PAN VEGETABLE CHOW MEIN WITH TOFU
CONTINUED

4 Place the baking sheet with the tofu on the bottom rack of the oven and the baking sheet with the vegetables on the middle rack. Bake for 10 minutes.

‼ 5 Meanwhile, place the noodles in a **large heatproof bowl**. Carefully add enough boiling water to cover the noodles. Let the noodles soak for 5 minutes, using **wooden chopsticks** or **tongs** to loosen them up. Ask a grown-up to drain the noodles in a **colander** in the sink. Rinse the noodles under cold water and drain again. Pat the noodles dry with a **clean kitchen towel**.

6 Return the noodles to the empty heatproof bowl. Drizzle them with the remaining 1 to 2 tablespoons neutral oil and sprinkle with 1 teaspoon salt and a big pinch of black or white pepper. Use the tongs to toss the noodles until they're well coated with the seasonings.

‼ 7 Use **oven mitts** to remove the baking sheets from the oven and place them on the stovetop or **two cooling racks**. Use a **spatula** to flip each piece of tofu over. On the vegetable baking sheet, push the veggies to the sides and add the noodles in the center, spreading them out as much as possible (be careful, the baking sheet is hot!).

8 Use oven mitts to return the baking sheets to the oven, switching them so the tofu is on the middle rack and the noodles and vegetables are on the bottom one. Bake until the tofu is golden and the noodles are crispy on the top and bottom, 10 to 15 minutes.

9 **For the seasoning sauce:** Meanwhile, in a **small bowl**, **whisk** together the stir-fry sauce, garlic, pepper, sesame oil, and soy sauce to combine.

‼ 10 Use oven mitts to remove both baking sheets from the oven and place them on the stovetop or the cooling racks. Pour the seasoning sauce over the noodles and toss well to coat. Transfer the tofu to the noodles and scatter the scallion and sesame seeds over top. Serve immediately in bowls.

Seasoning Sauce
1 tablespoon vegetarian stir-fry sauce or oyster sauce (for non-vegetarians)

1 small garlic clove, peeled and grated (see page 13)

Black or white pepper

1 tablespoon sesame oil (toasted or untoasted)

3 tablespoons soy sauce

1 scallion, trimmed and thinly sliced, for serving

Toasted white sesame seeds, for serving

SCISSOR-CUT NOODLES WITH KIMCHI

SERVES 4

Using kitchen shears to cut a simple dough into delightfully chewy noodles is super easy and super fun! This style of noodles, also called jian dao mian, is originally from Northern China. We toss the cooked noodles with some kimchi and a stir-together sauce, but you can add your favorite stir-fried veggies and/or meat and swap the sauce here.

1. In a **large bowl**, combine the flour, salt, and water. Use a **rubber spatula** to stir and press the ingredients until the dough comes together.

2. Sprinkle a clean counter with a little more flour. Transfer the dough to the floured counter. Knead the dough until it looks smooth and you can't see any dry flour, about 5 minutes. Use your hands to form the dough into a ball.

3. Place the dough ball back into the large bowl and cover the bowl with **plastic wrap**. Let the dough rest for 15 minutes.

4. While the dough is resting, in a **small bowl**, combine the soy sauce, vinegar, sugar, and garlic. Use a **spoon** to stir until combined.

5. Place a **colander** in the sink. Add the water to a **large pot** and bring it to a boil over high heat.

6. When the dough is ready, cut the noodles following the photos on pages 164–165.

‼ 7. Carefully add the noodles to the boiling water and cook, stirring occasionally with a **wooden spoon**, until they float and are tender, 5 to 7 minutes. Turn off the stovetop.

‼ 8. Ask a grown-up to carefully drain the noodles in the colander in the sink. Transfer the noodles to a **12-inch nonstick skillet**.

9. Add the kimchi and the soy sauce mixture to the skillet. Cook over medium heat, stirring occasionally, until the kimchi is warmed through, 3 to 4 minutes. Turn off the stovetop.

‼ 10. Carefully transfer the noodles to **serving bowls**. Sprinkle with the scallions. Serve.

INGREDIENTS

3 cups all-purpose flour, plus extra for kneading

1 teaspoon table salt

¾ cup plus 2 tablespoons water

¼ cup soy sauce

2 tablespoons unseasoned rice vinegar

1 teaspoon sugar

1 garlic clove, peeled and minced (see page 13)

4 quarts water

1½ cups kimchi

2 scallions, trimmed and sliced thin

FUN FOOD FACT

This style of noodle comes from Shanxi Province in China, where chefs slice noodles off big blocks of dough directly into boiling water. Shanxi was also home to the first and only woman to be emperor in Chinese history, Empress Wu Zetian.

HOW TO CUT NOODLES

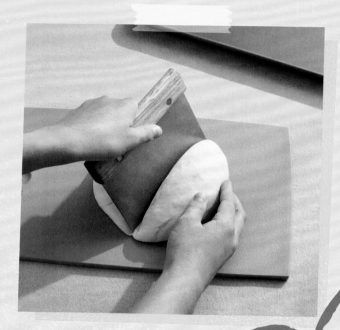

1

Remove the dough ball from the bowl and place it on a clean counter. Discard the plastic wrap. Use a **bench scraper** or **chef's knife** to cut the dough in half.

2

Pat each dough half into an 8-by-5-inch oval that is ½ to ¾ inch thick. (Don't worry about making the measurements perfect.)

3

Hold one dough oval over a rimmed baking sheet. Use kitchen shears to snip off 1½- to 2-inch pieces of dough, letting them fall onto the baking sheet. (It's totally fine if they're not exactly the same size or shape.)

YOU'RE THE CHEF

"These noodles were deliciously chewy."
—Goldie, age 11

GRANDMA PIZZA

INGREDIENTS

2 tablespoons extra-virgin olive oil

1 pound store-bought pizza dough

1 (14.5-ounce) can crushed tomatoes

1 garlic clove, peeled and minced (see page 13)

1 teaspoon dried oregano

½ teaspoon garlic powder

½ teaspoon red wine vinegar

½ teaspoon table salt

¼ teaspoon pepper

2 cups shredded mozzarella cheese (see page 16)

½ cup grated Parmesan cheese (see page 16)

¼ cup fresh basil leaves, chopped or torn (see page 10, optional)

Grandma Pizza is made in a rimmed baking sheet and topped with cheese and then tomato sauce, which might be the opposite of the pizza you're used to. It's said to have been invented by the children of Italian immigrants living on Long Island, New York. Make sure your pizza dough is at room temperature before starting this recipe—if the dough is cold, it will be very difficult to stretch.

1   Pour the oil onto a rimmed baking sheet and use your hands to spread it around to coat the entire pan.

2   Place the pizza dough on the greased baking sheet and flip it over to coat both sides of the dough in oil. Use your hands to gently pat and stretch the dough as close to the corners of the baking sheet as it will go without tearing. The dough will start to shrink back as you stretch—that's OK!

3   Cover the baking sheet with plastic wrap and let the dough rise at room temperature until it's bubbly and puffy, 30 to 40 minutes.

4   While the dough is rising, set an oven rack in the middle position and heat the oven to 450°F.

5   In a medium bowl, combine the crushed tomatoes, garlic, oregano, garlic powder, red wine vinegar, salt, and pepper. Use a large spoon to stir until well combined.

6   When the dough is ready, remove the plastic wrap. Pat and stretch the dough the rest of the way into the corners of the baking sheet. (If the dough is still shrinking back, cover it with plastic wrap and let it rest for an additional 10 minutes before trying again.)

7   Sprinkle the mozzarella and Parmesan evenly over the surface of the dough. Use the large spoon to dollop sauce on top of the cheese.

8   Place the baking sheet in the oven. Bake until the cheese is browned and the sauce is bubbling, 15 to 18 minutes.

!! 9   Use oven mitts to remove the baking sheet from the oven and place it on the stovetop or a cooling rack. Let the pizza cool for 5 minutes. Sprinkle the basil evenly over the pizza (if using).

!! 10   Use a spatula to loosen the edges of the pizza, then carefully slide it onto a cutting board (be careful—the baking sheet will still be hot!). Use a pizza wheel or chef's knife to cut the pizza into squares. Serve.

MEET CHEF SARAH THOMAS

Every time Sarah smells nutmeg or mace, it brings her back to her grandmother's house in Kerala, India. Nutmeg used to grow on the property, and she remembers waking up early with her grandma and gathering it from the still-damp ground. Then they'd spread everything they'd collected to dry in the sun before it was processed to make cooking spices.

After working in bars and restaurants as a sommelier, or wine expert, Sarah decided to try something different. She cofounded a company called Kalamata's Kitchen that introduces kids to the wonderful world of cooking through storybooks, dining guides, and recipes. She loves tasting new flavors from around the world and wants to encourage young people to do the same.

Sarah wishes that she'd been kinder to herself on her first attempts to make her mom's recipes when she was starting to cook. She says, "When you start trying to re-create dishes, they don't always taste exactly like you remember—but that doesn't mean they aren't good or aren't 'right' in their own way."

Sarah's Rebel Girls dinner party would come with a twist! She'd make some foods from Kerala for Lakshmibai (the Rani of Jhansi), Emily Brontë, and Eleanor Roosevelt, but she'd also ask each woman to bring a dish that means something special to them.

MOM'S DAL

"This dal recipe is the one I grew up eating and is definitely my mom's variation on a dish that has about one billion variations across South Asia and the diaspora. Many kinds of lentils or pulses can be used to make this recipe, though I typically use split yellow mung beans (yellow lentils and red lentils also work well). Some will take longer than others to cook. Use your intuition and taste as you go, till you get the texture you like." —Sarah Thomas

1 **For the dal:** Place a **colander** in the sink. Add the mung beans to the colander and rinse under cold running water. Shake the colander to drain the beans well. Transfer the beans to a **large bowl**, add water until they're fully covered, and let the beans soak for 10 minutes. (Leave the colander in the sink.)

2 When the beans are ready, drain them in the colander in the sink. Transfer the beans to a **large saucepan** and add 4 cups water. Bring to a boil over medium-high heat. Turn down the heat to medium-low and cook for 20 minutes, stirring occasionally with a **wooden spoon**, until the dal softens. (If the dal starts to stick to the bottom of the pot, turn down the heat to low.)

3 Stir in the turmeric and salt. Cook, stirring occasionally, until the dal is very soft but still somewhat holds its shape, 20 to 30 minutes. Turn off the stovetop. You can stop here, drizzle 1 tablespoon melted ghee over the top, and serve for a very mild version of this dish.

‼4 **For the tadka:** Place the chiles on a **cutting board**. Break off and discard the stems. Use a **paring knife** to carefully slit one side of each chile's skin (don't cut it all the way in half—you want the chile to stay whole but open it slightly).

‼5 Add the ghee to a **small nonstick skillet**. Heat the skillet on the stovetop over medium-high heat until the ghee is hot but not smoking (see page 17). Add the mustard seeds and cumin. As soon as the mustard seeds pop, carefully add the chiles, garlic, ginger, onion, and curry leaves (if using; be careful—the oil can spatter a bit when you add the curry leaves).

CONTINUED

INGREDIENTS

Dal

1 cup dried split yellow mung beans (see the introduction)

¼ teaspoon ground turmeric

1 teaspoon kosher salt

Tadka

2 Indian green chiles or serrano chiles

1 tablespoon ghee, coconut oil, or vegetable oil, plus more for serving

¼ teaspoon brown mustard seeds

½ teaspoon whole cumin seeds

1 teaspoon peeled and minced garlic (see page 13)

1 teaspoon peeled and minced fresh ginger

1 small onion, peeled and chopped (see page 11)

¼ cup curry leaves, stems removed (optional)

Cooked rice (page 176), for serving

MOM'S DAL
CONTINUED

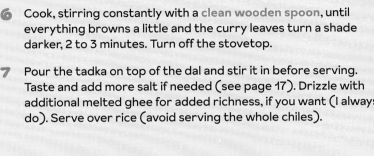

6 Cook, stirring constantly with a **clean wooden spoon**, until everything browns a little and the curry leaves turn a shade darker, 2 to 3 minutes. Turn off the stovetop.

7 Pour the tadka on top of the dal and stir it in before serving. Taste and add more salt if needed (see page 17). Drizzle with additional melted ghee for added richness, if you want (I always do). Serve over rice (avoid serving the whole chiles).

Sarah's proudest cooking accomplishment? "I'm just proud to know that I can take care of people with food. It's my way of showing love."

MEET CHEF PORTIA MBAU

Portia didn't like okra until she made it in an air fryer. When cooked this way, the vegetable, which she always found a little slimy, turned crispy and delicious.

When Portia was so small she couldn't reach the kitchen counter, her mother brought over a stool for her to stand on. Then she gave Portia a miniature rolling pin and her own set of kitchen utensils. Side by side, they baked.

When she grew up, Portia carried on the tradition with her own daughter, Lumai. When Lumai was young, she was nervous in the kitchen. The hot oven and sharp knives intimidated her. But as Portia and Lumai cooked together more and more, Lumai became more confident. The two women have the same taste in food—although neither likes doing the dishes!

In 1992, Portia opened the Africa Café, the first restaurant in South Africa that served African food. People came from all over to sample her delicious dishes, and soon, everyone wanted her recipes. So she put together a cookbook. She wrote the recipes, and Lumai took pictures.

Portia never went to cooking school—she learned from her mom, who made it seem easy. Other chefs talked about cooking like it was a complicated skill you needed to study to do professionally. Portia says, "I want everyone who loves to cook to know they can do it. You don't have to be classically trained to make amazing food."

If Portia were inviting three Rebels to dinner, she'd pick Maya Angelou, Winnie Mandela, and Tina Turner. She'd cook Ethiopian sik sik wat, a hearty beef stew in a sweet paprika sauce. Then they'd have cheesecake for dessert—Lumai's specialty!

SOUTH AFRICAN PEANUT AND GREENS STEW

SERVES 2 AS A MAIN
COURSE OR 4 AS A SIDE DISH

"You're in for a surprise with this simple stew. Peanut soup is a popular dish in South and East African cuisines. I tasted it many times in my travels in South Africa and Tanzania, and it reminded me of the creamed spinach my mom used to make. I created this recipe by combining my children's much-loved peanut butter and a healthy green vegetable: spinach. It's creamy and a little bit sweet, it's packed with iron and protein, and it tastes decadent and smooth—the perfect way to get more spinach into your meals. Feel free to use a chile of your choice to bring the spice level up or down. For peanut allergies, you can replace the peanut oil with olive oil and the peanut butter with cashew or almond butter. My family loves to eat this with mashed potatoes and gravy or rice and roast chicken." —Portia Mbau

INGREDIENTS

1 pound fresh mature curly leaf spinach

¼ cup peanut oil or olive oil

1 cup chopped onion (see page 11)

½ cup unsweetened desiccated (dried) coconut

½ teaspoon table salt

1 teaspoon seeded and finely chopped habanero chile (about ½ chile, see page 12)

1 cup coconut milk

¼ cup creamy peanut butter

1 Place a **colander** in the sink. Wash the spinach thoroughly under cold running water. Shake the colander to drain the spinach well. Repeat several times, then use your hands to tear the spinach into 1-inch pieces.

2 Add the oil to a **large pot** or **Dutch oven**. Heat the pot on the stovetop over medium heat until the oil is hot but not smoking (see page 17). Add the onions and cook, stirring frequently with a **wooden spoon**, until golden brown, about 10 minutes.

3 Reduce the heat to low. Add the coconut, salt, and habanero and cook, stirring frequently, for 5 minutes.

4 In a **small bowl**, use a **whisk** to mix the coconut milk and peanut butter until smooth.

5 Add the coconut milk mixture and the torn spinach to the pot. Cover the pot with a **lid**. Cook, stirring occasionally, until the spinach is wilted, about 15 minutes. Turn off the stovetop. Serve.

SERVES 4 (MAKES ABOUT 3 CUPS LONG-GRAIN WHITE RICE OR BROWN RICE, ABOUT 2 CUPS SHORT-GRAIN WHITE RICE, SUSHI RICE, OR SHORT-GRAIN BROWN RICE)

TWO WAYS TO COOK RICE

There are two main ways to cook rice: You can steam it, or you can boil it and drain it, like cooking pasta. Steaming works great for white rice, and boiling brown rice is easy-peasy. Serve your cooked rice as a side dish—amp up the flavor by stirring in chopped fresh herbs, lemon or lime juice, and/or grated Parmesan cheese right before serving.

LONG-GRAIN WHITE RICE INGREDIENTS

1 cup long-grain white rice

2 cups water

½ teaspoon table salt

SHORT-GRAIN WHITE RICE OR SUSHI RICE INGREDIENTS

1 cup short-grain white rice or sushi rice

1¼ cups water

¼ teaspoon table salt

LONG-GRAIN OR SHORT-GRAIN BROWN RICE INGREDIENTS

2 quarts water

1 cup long-grain or short-grain brown rice

1½ teaspoons table salt

FOR LONG-GRAIN WHITE RICE, SHORT-GRAIN WHITE RICE, OR SUSHI RICE

1   Place a **fine-mesh strainer** in the sink. Add the rice to the strainer. Rinse the rice under cold running water until the water runs clear, 1 to 2 minutes. Shake the strainer to drain the rice well.

2   In a **medium saucepan**, combine the rice, water, and salt.

3   Bring the water to a boil over medium-high heat. Reduce the heat to low, cover the saucepan with a **lid**, and cook for 20 minutes.

4   Turn off the stovetop and carefully slide the saucepan to a cool burner. Let the rice sit, covered, to finish cooking, 5 minutes for long-grain white rice or 10 minutes for short-grain white rice or sushi rice.

5   Use **oven mitts** to remove the lid. Serve.

FOR LONG-GRAIN OR SHORT-GRAIN BROWN RICE

1   Add the water to a **large pot**. Bring to a boil over medium-high heat.

!! 2   Carefully add the rice and salt to the boiling water. Cook, stirring occasionally with a **wooden spoon**, until the rice is tender, 25 to 35 minutes.

!! 3   When the rice is ready, turn off the stovetop. Ask a grown-up to drain the rice in a **fine-mesh strainer** in the sink.

4   Use the wooden spoon to transfer the rice to a **serving bowl**. Serve.

FOR EXTRA FLAVOR, TOAST YOUR LONG-GRAIN WHITE RICE

For an extra-flavorful side dish, toast your long-grain white rice before you steam it. Before you add the rice, water, and salt, melt 2 tablespoons unsalted butter in the medium saucepan over medium-low heat. Add the rice and salt and cook, stirring frequently with a wooden spoon, until the rice is toasted and fragrant (it will smell a little bit nutty), about 2 minutes. Add the water and continue the recipe at step 3.

ROASTED VEGGIES

LEMONY ROASTED BROCCOLI INGREDIENTS

1 pound broccoli florets, large florets cut in half (about 7 cups)

¼ cup extra-virgin olive oil

Zest of ½ lemon (see page 15), plus lemon wedges for serving

½ teaspoon table salt

Pinch of pepper

HONEY-BUTTER ROASTED CARROTS INGREDIENTS

1½ pounds carrots, peeled and cut the short way into ½-inch-thick slices

2 tablespoons honey

2 tablespoons unsalted butter, cut into small pieces

1 tablespoon extra-virgin olive oil

½ teaspoon table salt

GARLICKY ROASTED POTATOES INGREDIENTS

1½ pounds small red or yellow potatoes or fingerling potatoes, cut in half (or left whole if very small)

2 tablespoons extra-virgin olive oil

1 teaspoon garlic powder

½ teaspoon onion powder

½ teaspoon table salt

Pinch of pepper

Roasting vegetables in the oven makes them extra delicious! As they brown, they form lots of delicious new flavor compounds thanks to some tasty chemistry. It's important to cut your veggies into similar size pieces so they cook evenly—so pay attention as you prep. If you like, you can dress up your roasted veggies before serving with a sprinkle of grated Parmesan cheese and/or chopped fresh herbs, such as parsley, chives, or rosemary.

1 Set an oven rack in the middle position and heat the oven to 450°F. Line a **rimmed baking sheet** with **parchment paper**.

2 Combine all the ingredients for your roasted veggie of choice in a **large bowl**. Use a **rubber spatula** to stir until the vegetables are evenly coated with the oil and seasonings.

3 Transfer the mixture to the parchment-lined baking sheet. Spread everything into an even layer and turn the vegetables cut-side down.

4 Place the baking sheet in the oven. Bake until the vegetables are tender and browned on the bottom, 10 to 15 minutes for broccoli, 20 to 25 minutes for carrots, and 25 to 30 minutes for potatoes.

‼5 Use **oven mitts** to remove the baking sheet from the oven and place it on the stovetop or a **cooling rack**. Let cool slightly, about 5 minutes. Use a **spatula** to transfer the vegetables to a **serving bowl**. Taste and season with a little extra salt and pepper if desired (see page 17). Serve (with lemon wedges, if making Lemony Roasted Broccoli).

SHAKE-iT-UP SALAD DRESSiNGS

MAKES ABOUT ¾ CUP SALAD DRESSiNG

"Shake things up" with one of these three easy and delicious salad dressings. Just add your ingredients to a jar, screw on the lid, and shake, shake, shake until the ingredients are combined. Salad dressing dance parties are encouraged!

1 Combine all the ingredients for your dressing of choice in a **small jar**. Cover the jar tightly with a **lid**.

2 Shake the jar until the ingredients are well combined, 30 seconds to 1 minute.

3 Drizzle about 2 tablespoons of the dressing over each serving of your favorite salad. (Extra dressing can be stored in the jar in the refrigerator for up to 3 days. Shake the jar to recombine the ingredients before serving.)

EVERYDAY ViNAiGRETTE iNGREDiENTS

¼ cup extra-virgin olive oil

1 small garlic clove, peeled and minced (see page 13)

1½ tablespoons lemon juice (see page 15)

¾ teaspoon Dijon mustard

1½ teaspoons water

Salt and pepper

YOGURT-HERB DRESSiNG iNGREDiENTS

3 tablespoons plain yogurt

2 tablespoons chopped fresh parsley, basil, or cilantro leaves (or a mix, see page 10)

2 tablespoons extra-virgin olive oil

2 teaspoons lemon or lime juice (see page 15)

Salt and pepper

TAHiNi-SOY DRESSiNG iNGREDiENTS

2 tablespoons tahini

1 tablespoon soy sauce

1 tablespoon mayonnaise

1 tablespoon water

1 teaspoon rice vinegar

MAKES 4 FLATBREADS

STOVETOP FLATBREADS

INGREDIENTS

2 cups (10 ounces) all-purpose flour, plus extra for the counter

¼ teaspoon instant or rapid-rise yeast

¾ cup water

3 tablespoons plus 2 teaspoons extra-virgin olive oil, measured separately

1 teaspoon table salt

These tender-but-chewy flatbreads are cooked on the stovetop—not in the oven—and are the perfect partner for soups, stews, curries, and more. Don't worry if your flatbreads are all slightly different shapes—they'll still taste great!

1. Add the flour and yeast to a food processor. Lock the lid into place and process until well combined, about 5 seconds. Stop the processor.

2. Combine the water and 3 tablespoons of the oil in a liquid measuring cup. With the processor running, add the oil and water mixture through the processor's feed tube. Process until the dough forms a ball and no longer sticks to the sides of the processor bowl, 30 seconds to 1 minute. Stop the processor.

3. Let the dough sit in the processor for 5 minutes. (This gives the flour time to fully absorb all the liquid and will make for a softer dough that is easier to work with.)

4. While the dough is resting, add the remaining 2 teaspoons oil to a medium bowl and swirl it around to coat the sides.

!! 5. When the dough is ready, remove the lid from the processor and add the salt. Lock the lid back into place and process until the salt is mixed in and the dough is smooth, about 1 minute. Remove the lid and carefully remove the processor blade.

6. Sprinkle a clean counter with a little flour and coat your hands with flour. Transfer the dough to the floured counter and form it into a ball. Place the dough into the greased bowl.

7. Cover the bowl with plastic wrap. Let the dough rise at room temperature until it looks puffy, 30 to 45 minutes.

CONTINUED

8 When the dough is ready, sprinkle the counter with a little flour. Place the risen dough on the lightly floured counter and use a **bench scraper** or a **chef's knife** to cut it into 4 equal pieces. Cover the dough pieces loosely with **plastic wrap**. Shape 4 flatbreads following the photos on the opposite page.

9 Heat a **10-inch skillet** over medium heat until hot but not smoking, about 2 minutes.

‼ 10 Carefully place 1 flatbread in the skillet and cook until the bottom is spotty brown, 1 to 3 minutes (to check: slide a **spatula** underneath the flatbread and lift up a little bit to peek underneath).

11 Use the spatula to carefully flip the flatbread and cook until the second side is spotty brown, 1 to 3 minutes. If the skillet starts to smoke, or the flatbreads are cooking too fast, turn down the heat to low.

12 Carefully transfer the flatbread to a **large plate** and cover it with a **clean dish towel** to keep it warm. Turn down the heat to medium-low. Repeat with the remaining 3 flatbreads. Turn off the stovetop. Serve the flatbreads warm.

FLAVORED FLATBREADS

Flatbread with Herbs

Add ⅓ cup roughly chopped cilantro, parsley, or basil leaves (see page 10) to the food processor in step 1 with the flour and yeast.

Za'atar Flatbread

Add 2 teaspoons za'atar to the food processor in step 1 with the flour and yeast.

HOW TO SHAPE FLATBREADS

1

Working with 1 piece of dough at a time (keep the other pieces of dough covered with plastic wrap), use your hands to tuck the corners of the dough into the center to form a round shape. Pinch the edges together.

2

Flip the dough over and use your hands to pat and stretch it into a rough 7-inch circle. (If the dough keeps pulling back when you try to stretch it, cover the dough loosely with plastic wrap and let it rest for 5 minutes before trying again.) Repeat to shape the remaining pieces of dough.

KOREAN CORN CHEESE

This Korean American side dish is the perfect balance of creamy, savory, and sweet. Gochugaru is a Korean chile powder—look for it in the spice aisle of your grocery store, in East Asian markets, or online. You can use a 15-ounce can of corn kernels, drained, or the kernels cut from 4 ears of fresh corn instead of the frozen corn.

1. Set an oven rack in the upper-middle position and heat the oven to 400°F.

2. In a **large bowl,** combine the corn, bell pepper, mayonnaise, sugar, salt, pepper, and cheese. Use a **rubber spatula** to stir until well combined.

3. Use the rubber spatula to transfer the corn mixture to an **8-by-8-inch square baking dish** and smooth the top.

4. Place the baking dish in the oven. Bake until the cheese is bubbling, about 15 minutes.

‼ 5. Use **oven mitts** to remove the baking dish from the oven and place it on the stovetop or a **cooling rack.** Let the mixture cool slightly, about 5 minutes.

6. Sprinkle with the sliced scallion and gochugaru (if using). Serve warm.

INGREDIENTS

4 cups (16 ounces) frozen corn, thawed

½ red bell pepper, chopped

¼ cup mayonnaise

1 teaspoon granulated sugar

¼ teaspoon table salt

⅛ teaspoon black pepper

1 cup shredded mozzarella cheese (see page 16)

1 scallion, trimmed and sliced thin

¼ teaspoon gochugaru (optional)

REBEL IN THE KITCHEN

Corn cheese is a common side dish for Korean barbecue. Chef Lauren Kim runs a Korean barbecue restaurant in Thailand— one of seven restaurants she's opened.

CUCUMBER RIBBON SALAD

INGREDIENTS

1 English cucumber

½ teaspoon table salt

2 tablespoons unseasoned rice vinegar

1 teaspoon toasted sesame oil

¾ teaspoon granulated sugar

½ teaspoon sesame seeds (optional)

A trusty vegetable peeler is all you need to make fancy-looking cucumber ribbons. (You can use the same technique with carrots, zucchini, and summer squash, too.) English cucumbers have dense flesh and not that many seeds inside, which makes them easier to turn into ribbons. They're often sold shrink-wrapped in plastic at the grocery store. Don't substitute American or Persian cucumbers here, as their insides will be too wet and seedy to turn into ribbons.

1   Place the cucumber on a **cutting board** and trim the ends with a **chef's knife**. Discard the ends. Cut the cucumber in half the short way.

2   Hold one piece of cucumber flat on the cutting board using the hand you *don't* write with. Use a **vegetable peeler** to peel off a thin strip along the top, moving from end to end. Discard the first strip (it will be all peel!). Repeat peeling from end to end to make thin ribbons. When you get halfway through the cucumber, flip it over and repeat peeling until you get to the bottom. Repeat with the second piece of cucumber.

3   Place the cucumber ribbons in a **large bowl** and sprinkle them with the salt. Use a **rubber spatula** to stir until the cucumbers are evenly coated. Let sit for 10 minutes (this helps pull some of the water out of the cucumber, so your salad will be crunchy, not soggy).

4   While the cucumbers are sitting, in a **small bowl**, **whisk** the vinegar, sesame oil, and sugar until the sugar has dissolved.

5   When the cucumbers are ready, use **tongs** to transfer the ribbons to a **serving bowl**, gently shaking off the extra liquid and leaving behind the liquid in the bowl. Pour the dressing over the cucumbers and use the tongs to gently toss to combine. Sprinkle with the sesame seeds (if using) and serve.

OVEN-ROASTED MADUROS
SWEET PLANTAINS

SERVES 4

Golden brown on the outside, creamy on the inside, maduros are made with sweet, very ripe plantains. They're a popular side dish throughout Latin America and the Caribbean. Plantains turn from green to yellow to black as they ripen. Be sure to use very ripe plantains in this recipe—look for ones that are fully black.

INGREDIENTS

3 very ripe medium plantains (about 10 ounces total)

1 tablespoon extra-virgin olive oil

½ teaspoon table salt

1 Set an oven rack in the middle position and heat the oven to 450°F. Line a **rimmed baking sheet** with **parchment paper**.

2 Place the plantains on a **cutting board**. Use a **chef's knife** to cut off the ends of each plantain. Discard the ends. Slice each plantain the long way to split the peel open, making sure not to cut into the flesh. Use your hands to peel back the skin of each plantain until it's completely removed. Discard the skins. Cut each plantain the short way into 8 pieces, cutting at an angle (this is also called cutting "on the bias").

3 Place the plantain slices on the prepared baking sheet. Drizzle the oil over the plantain slices and sprinkle them with the salt. Use your hands to toss until the plantains are evenly coated. Spread the slices into an even layer on the baking sheet.

4 Place the baking sheet in the oven. Bake until the first side is golden brown, 5 to 7 minutes.

!! 5 Use **oven mitts** to remove the baking sheet from the oven and place it on the stovetop or a **cooling rack**. Use a **spatula** to flip the plantains over.

!! 6 Use oven mitts to return the baking sheet to the oven and bake until the second side is golden brown, 5 to 7 minutes.

!! 7 Use oven mitts to remove the baking sheet from the oven and place it on the stovetop or cooling rack. Serve.

YOU'RE THE CHEF
"I liked the combo of salty and sweet." –Linnea, age 12

DESSERTS

THICK AND CHEWY CHOCOLATE CHIP COOKIES

INGREDIENTS

2 cups bread flour

¾ teaspoon baking soda

¾ teaspoon table salt

1½ sticks (12 tablespoons) unsalted butter, melted and cooled

1 large egg plus 1 large egg yolk (see page 17)

1½ teaspoons vanilla extract

1 cup packed dark brown sugar

¼ cup granulated sugar

1 cup semisweet chocolate chips

You can bake these cookies in two batches, one baking sheet at a time, or you can freeze the second batch after shaping the cookies. Cover the baking sheet in plastic wrap and freeze for about 2 hours. Once the dough balls are frozen, transfer them to a zipper-lock plastic bag and store in the freezer for up to 1 month. Bake the dough from frozen, adding 2 to 3 minutes to the baking time. Bread flour will give you the thickest, chewiest cookies, but you can use 2 cups of all-purpose flour instead, if that's what you have on hand.

1   In a large bowl, whisk together the flour, baking soda, and salt.

2   In a medium bowl, whisk together the melted butter, egg, egg yolk, and vanilla until combined.

3   Add the brown sugar and granulated sugar to the butter mixture and whisk until smooth.

4   Add the butter mixture to the flour mixture and use a rubber spatula to stir until the dough is combined and you can't see any bits of dry flour.

5   Add the chocolate chips to the dough and stir until just combined. Place the bowl in the refrigerator and chill the dough for 30 minutes.

6   Meanwhile, set an oven rack in the middle position and heat the oven to 325°F. Line two rimmed baking sheets with parchment paper.

7   When the dough is chilled, use a 1-tablespoon measuring spoon to divide the dough into heaping 1-tablespoon portions. Use slightly wet hands to roll the dough portions into balls and place them on the prepared baking sheets, 12 balls per sheet. (Leave some space in between the dough balls.)

8   Place one baking sheet in the oven and bake until the cookies are golden brown, 10 to 12 minutes.

CONTINUED

THICK AND CHEWY
CHOCOLATE CHIP COOKIES
CONTINUED

 9 Use **oven mitts** to remove the baking sheet from the oven and place it on the stovetop or a **cooling rack**. Bake the second batch (or freeze those dough balls, see the introduction). Let the cookies cool completely on the baking sheet, about 30 minutes. Serve.

THIN AND CRISPY CHOCOLATE CHIP COOKIES

Like your cookies crispy instead of chewy? Try these tweaks: Swap in 2¾ cups cake flour for the bread flour. (Don't have cake flour? You can use 2 cups all-purpose flour instead—your cookies will be a little less thin and crispy, but still delicious.) Increase the granulated sugar to ¾ cup. Use ½ cup packed light brown sugar instead of the dark brown sugar. Use mini chocolate chips instead of regular-size chips. In step 7, use a lightly wet hand to gently press each portion of dough into a 2-inch-wide circle (no need to roll the dough into balls first). Increase the baking time to 13 to 15 minutes.

 ### REBEL IN THE KITCHEN

In the 1930s, Ruth Wakefield opened the Toll House Inn, where she served chocolate chip cookies that people couldn't get enough of. When she published the recipe in her cookbook, the candy company Nestlé saw a huge jump in sales of their chocolate bars and asked if they could print her cookie recipe on the back of their wrappers. They even created the chip-shaped morsels we use today so people wouldn't need to chop up the chocolate by hand.

PEANUT BUTTER COOKIES

This recipe works best with a processed peanut butter, such as Skippy or Jif. Natural peanut butters have a different consistency that will affect the texture of the dough. Dark brown sugar gives these cookies a boost of caramel flavor, but you can use light brown sugar if that's what you have on hand.

1 Set an oven rack in the middle position and heat the oven to 350°F. Line two **rimmed baking sheets** with **parchment paper**.

2 Add the peanuts to a **zipper-lock bag**, press out all of the air, and seal the bag. Lay the bag flat on the counter and use a **rolling pin** to gently crush the peanuts into small pieces. Set aside.

3 In a **medium bowl**, **whisk** together the flour, baking soda, baking powder, and salt.

4 Add the butter, brown sugar, and granulated sugar to a **large bowl** (if you're using a handheld mixer) or the bowl of a **stand mixer** fitted with the **paddle attachment** (if you're using a stand mixer). Beat on medium speed until the ingredients are creamy and fluffy, about 3 minutes. Stop the mixer.

5 Use a **rubber spatula** to scrape down the sides of the bowl. Add the peanut butter, egg, and vanilla. Beat on medium speed until everything is fully incorporated, about 30 seconds. Stop the mixer.

6 Scrape down the sides of the bowl. Add half of the flour mixture. Beat on low speed until combined, about 30 seconds. Stop the mixer, then add the remaining flour mixture and beat on low speed until fully combined, about 30 seconds. Stop the mixer. Remove the paddle or beaters and scrape any dough sticking to them into the bowl.

INGREDIENTS

½ cup salted dry-roasted peanuts

1¼ cups all-purpose flour

½ teaspoon baking soda

¼ teaspoon baking powder

½ teaspoon table salt

8 tablespoons unsalted butter, cut into 8 pieces and softened

½ cup packed dark brown sugar

½ cup granulated sugar

½ cup creamy or crunchy peanut butter

1 large egg

1 teaspoon vanilla extract

CONTINUED

7   Add the crushed peanuts. Use the rubber spatula to stir until the peanuts are evenly distributed and no dry flour remains (make sure to scrape along the bottom and sides of the bowl).

8   Use a **1-tablespoon measuring spoon** to scoop twelve 1½-tablespoon portions of dough onto one of the parchment-lined baking sheets, leaving space between the portions. Use a **spoon** or **small rubber spatula** to help scoop the dough out of the measuring spoon and onto the baking sheet.

9   Fill a **small bowl** with water. Dip a **fork** into the water, then gently press down with the back of the fork onto the top of each dough ball (dip the fork in the water again as needed if the dough starts to stick). Repeat pressing in the opposite direction to make a crisscross pattern on the top of each dough ball (the cookies should be about ½ inch thick after pressing).

10   Place the baking sheet in the oven. Bake until the edges of the cookies are set and the middles are puffy, 11 to 13 minutes.

11   Meanwhile, repeat steps 8 and 9 to shape the remaining dough into cookies on the second parchment-lined baking sheet.

!! 12   When the first batch of cookies is ready, use **oven mitts** to remove the baking sheet from the oven and place it on the stovetop or a **cooling rack**. Let the cookies cool completely on the baking sheet before serving, about 30 minutes.

13   Bake the second batch of cookies or cover the second baking sheet with plastic wrap and freeze (see the introduction on page 194).

FUDGY BROWNIES

Dutch-processed cocoa powder gives these brownies their chewy texture and deep brown color. If you use natural cocoa powder, your brownies will turn out drier and lighter brown. We know it's hard to wait until brownies are fully cool to dig in, but this step is another part of the secret to their fudginess!

INGREDIENTS

Vegetable oil spray

3 tablespoons unsalted butter, melted and cooled (see page 17)

7 tablespoons vegetable oil

2 large eggs

1½ cups granulated sugar

½ cup unsweetened Dutch-processed cocoa powder

1 cup all-purpose flour

¼ teaspoon table salt

⅓ cup semisweet chocolate chips

1 Set an oven rack in the middle position and heat the oven to 325°F. Line an **8-by-8-inch square baking pan** with **aluminum foil**, letting some foil hang over the sides of the pan. Spray the foil evenly with vegetable oil spray.

2 In a **large bowl**, **whisk** the butter, oil, and eggs until combined.

3 Add the sugar, cocoa powder, flour, and salt and whisk until well combined and you can't see any dry cocoa powder or flour.

4 Add the chocolate chips to the bowl. Use a **rubber spatula** to stir until the chips are incorporated into the batter.

5 Scrape the batter into the prepared baking pan and smooth the top.

6 Place the baking pan in the oven. Bake until a toothpick inserted into the center comes out with only a few crumbs attached, 30 to 35 minutes.

!! 7 Use **oven mitts** to remove the baking pan from the oven and place it on the stovetop or a **cooling rack**. Let the brownies cool completely in the pan, about 1 hour.

8 Use the edges of the foil to carefully lift the brownies out of the baking pan and place them on a **cutting board**. Cut the brownies into squares and serve.

 FUN FOOD FACT

It's believed the first mention of brownies in a cookbook was way back in 1906 . . . and the recipe didn't include chocolate. That recipe, written by chef Fannie Farmer, was for a molasses cookie. Ten years later, Fannie published a brownie recipe with chocolate, but it still wasn't as chocolaty as this one!

CHOCOLATE SHEET CAKE

INGREDIENTS

Vegetable oil spray

2 sticks
(16 tablespoons)
unsalted butter,
cut into 16 pieces

1 cup water

⅔ cup unsweetened
Dutch-processed
cocoa powder

2½ cups all-purpose
flour

2 cups granulated
sugar

1 teaspoon baking
powder

¼ teaspoon baking
soda

½ teaspoon table salt

⅔ cup buttermilk

2 large eggs

1 teaspoon vanilla
extract

3 cups frosting
(see the introduction)

Frost this cake with homemade Vanilla Buttercream Frosting (page 205, or your favorite store-bought frosting) and decorate it with colorful sprinkles or sanding sugar. Dutch-processed cocoa powder keeps this cake extra moist and chocolaty. Look for brands such as Droste, Valrhona, or Guittard. You can use natural unsweetened cocoa powder (like Hershey's), but the cake will be drier and more crumbly—and also lighter brown.

1. Set an oven rack in the middle position and heat the oven to 350°F. Spray the inside of a 9-by-13-inch metal baking pan with vegetable oil spray.

2. In a medium saucepan, combine the butter, water, and cocoa powder. Place the saucepan on the stovetop over medium heat. Cook, stirring occasionally with a rubber spatula, until the butter is melted and the mixture is just beginning to bubble, 5 to 7 minutes. Turn off the stovetop and slide the saucepan to a cool burner. Let cool slightly, about 10 minutes.

3. While the cocoa mixture is cooling, in a large bowl, whisk together the flour, sugar, baking powder, baking soda, and salt.

4. Pour the buttermilk into a liquid measuring cup. Crack the eggs into the same measuring cup. Add the vanilla and use a fork to lightly beat until just combined.

5. When the cocoa mixture has cooled, use the rubber spatula to scrape it into the bowl with the flour mixture. Stir gently until just combined and you can't see any bits of dry flour (make sure to scrape along the bottom and sides of the bowl as you stir).

6. Add the buttermilk mixture and whisk until the batter is evenly combined. Use the rubber spatula to scrape the batter into the greased baking pan.

7. Place the baking pan in the oven. Bake until the cake is puffy and shiny and a toothpick inserted into the center of the cake comes out clean, 32 to 36 minutes.

CONTINUED

!!8 Use **oven mitts** to remove the baking pan from the oven and place it on the stovetop or a **cooling rack**. Let the cake cool completely in the pan, at least 2 hours.

9 Use a **butter knife** to loosen the edges of the cake from the pan. Use an **offset spatula** or the butter knife to spread the frosting in an even layer over the top of the cake. Cut the cake into pieces and serve.

CHOCOLATE CUPCAKES

To make this recipe into 12 cupcakes instead of a sheet cake, cut the amounts of all the ingredients in half. Use a **12-cup muffin tin** lined with **12 paper cupcake liners** instead of the baking pan. In step 2, reduce the cooking time to 3 to 4 minutes. Divide the batter evenly among the cupcake liners, filling them to about ½ inch from the top. Reduce the baking time to 16 to 18 minutes. After the cupcakes are fully cool, remove them from the muffin tin and use a **small offset spatula**, **butter knife**, or **piping bag** to frost the top of each cupcake.

 FUN FOOD FACT

When famous singer Celia Cruz won her first singing competition, the prize was a cake! Celia went on to make salsa music popular in the United States, recording more than 80 albums and winning seven Grammys.

VANILLA BUTTERCREAM FROSTING

MAKES 3 CUPS FROSTING

INGREDIENTS

2½ sticks (20 tablespoons) unsalted butter, cut into 20 pieces and softened

2½ cups (10 ounces) confectioners' (powdered) sugar

2 teaspoons vanilla extract

¼ teaspoon table salt

⅓ cup heavy cream

Food coloring (optional)

Use liquid or gel food coloring to create colorful frosting. Add just a little bit at a time—the color might come out darker than you expect. You can also swap the vanilla extract for other flavors, such as peppermint, coconut, orange, or raspberry. Use just ½ teaspoon of these flavors, since they're much stronger than vanilla.

1. Add the butter to a **large bowl** (if you're using a handheld mixer) or the bowl of a **stand mixer** fitted with the paddle attachment (if you're using a stand mixer). With the mixer running on low speed, slowly add the confectioners' sugar, a little bit at a time, and beat the mixture on low speed until all of the sugar has been incorporated, 1 to 2 minutes. Stop the mixer.

2. Use a **rubber spatula** to scrape down the sides of the bowl and the beaters or paddle. Add the vanilla and salt. Beat on medium speed until the frosting is light and fluffy, about 5 minutes, stopping the mixer and scraping down the sides of the bowl and the paddle or beaters with the rubber spatula a couple of times along the way. Stop the mixer.

3. Scrape down the sides of the bowl. Add the cream and food coloring (if using). Beat on low speed until the cream is fully incorporated, 30 seconds to 1 minute. Increase the speed to medium and beat until fluffy, about 30 seconds. Stop the mixer.

4. Remove the paddle or beaters and scrape any frosting from them into the bowl. Gently stir the frosting one more time. Time to frost your cake or cupcakes.

STICKY TOFFEE PUDDING MUG CAKE

INGREDIENTS

¼ cup chopped pitted dates

1 tablespoon water

1 tablespoon unsalted butter, cut into 4 pieces

⅛ teaspoon baking soda

1 egg

¼ teaspoon vanilla extract

1 tablespoon plus 2 tablespoons packed dark brown sugar, measured separately

1½ teaspoons plus 2 tablespoons heavy cream, measured separately

¼ cup all-purpose flour

¼ teaspoon baking powder

Table salt

Sticky toffee pudding is a dessert that originated in England and is beloved throughout Great Britain, Australia, and New Zealand. This cake (yes, it's a cake, not a pudding!) is made with dates and brown sugar and is typically baked or steamed in the oven. Then, a caramelly toffee sauce is poured over the top. This version makes an individual portion in the microwave in less than 10 minutes, so you can enjoy this British treat anytime. Make sure the mug you use holds at least 12 ounces (or 1½ cups) so it doesn't overflow and make a mess in the microwave.

1   In a **12-ounce microwave-safe mug**, combine the dates and water. Heat in the microwave until the water is bubbling and the mixture is steaming, about 1 minute.

2   Use **oven mitts** to remove the mug from the microwave. Use a **spoon** to stir in the butter pieces and the baking soda (the mixture will fizz a little bit). Let sit for 1 minute to let the butter melt and the dates soften.

3   Crack the egg into a **small bowl** and use a **fork** to beat it until it's a uniform yellow color. Measure out 2 tablespoons of the beaten egg and add it to the mug. (Discard the rest of the egg or use it to make a second mug cake for a friend or family member.) Add the vanilla, 1 tablespoon of the brown sugar, and 1½ teaspoons of the cream and stir the mixture until well combined.

4   Add the flour, baking powder, and a pinch of salt and stir until well combined and you can't see any bits of dry flour.

5   In a **second small bowl**, use a **clean spoon** to stir together the remaining 2 tablespoons brown sugar, 2 tablespoons cream, and a pinch of salt. Pour the sugar mixture on top of the cake batter in the mug.

6   Heat the mug in the microwave until the cake has risen and is firm on top but the sauce is still liquid, 1 to 1½ minutes. Use oven mitts to remove the mug from the microwave and let it cool for 1 minute. Enjoy!

MEET CHEF REYNA DƯƠNG

When Reyna was five, she would drag a kitchen chair over to the sink so she could reach the faucet. From up there, she'd wash a large colander of bean sprouts. It was the first step to making her favorite meal—bean sprouts with white rice and fish sauce.

Now Reyna runs two restaurants in Dallas, Texas: Sandwich Hag, a banh mi restaurant, and Chimlanh, a coffee shop. She is also the culinary director at Hugs Cafe, a nonprofit that teaches adults with developmental disabilities skills for entering the food industry. She serves Vietnamese food that she describes as "savory, vibrant, and comforting." In her restaurants, she hires workers with disabilities, like her brother Sang, who has Down syndrome. Sang is Reyna's favorite person to cook with.

Reyna is proud of being a leader in the male-dominated cooking industry. In everything she does, she strives to support other women-owned businesses and entrepreneurs. By doing so, she creates a strong example for the women and girls in her community.

Reyna's guests of honor at a Rebel Girls dinner party would be Maya Angelou and Reyna's Má. She'd serve three types of Xíu Mai, a type of Vietnamese meatball.

VIETNAMESE COCONUT TOAST

INGREDIENTS

3 Vietnamese baguettes (see the introduction)

17 ounces unsweetened coconut cream (see the introduction)

5 tablespoons granulated sugar

½ cup sweetened shredded coconut

½ cup unsalted dry-roasted peanuts

1 teaspoon sesame seeds

1 teaspoon kosher salt

½ cup condensed milk, at room temperature

"Growing up, I would snack on baguettes and condensed milk all the time. My Vietnamese Coconut Toast is a fun twist on a childhood favorite that I introduced to my wonderful community of customers at Sandwich Hag, my restaurant in Dallas, Texas. It's the perfect balance of thin, crunchy bread that's slightly sweet with a touch of salt. Look for Vietnamese baguettes in a Vietnamese bakery or an Asian supermarket. If you can't find them, you can use one soft French baguette, or one or two Mexican bolillos or Cubano rolls. Be sure to use canned unsweetened coconut cream, not cream of coconut, which will make this dessert way too sweet. Longevity Brand is my favorite for condensed milk if you can find it!" —Reyna Dương

1   Set an oven rack in the highest position and heat the oven to 350°F.

2   Place the baguettes on a **cutting board**. Use a **bread knife** to slice the baguettes on an angle into sixteen to twenty 1-inch-thick slices.

3   In a **small saucepan**, combine the coconut cream and sugar. Bring the mixture to a low simmer (small bubbles appear all over the surface) on the stovetop over medium heat. Cook, stirring frequently with a **wooden spoon**, until the sugar dissolves. Turn off the stovetop and slide the saucepan to a cool burner.

4   Add the shredded coconut to a **10-inch skillet**. Cook over medium heat, stirring frequently with a **clean wooden spoon**, until the coconut is light golden brown. Turn off the stovetop. Carefully transfer the coconut to a **large plate**.

5   Add the peanuts to the empty skillet. Cook over medium heat, stirring frequently with the wooden spoon, until you start to see some brown spots appear on the peanuts. Add the sesame seeds to the skillet and cook, stirring frequently, until the sesame seeds turn light golden brown, 1 to 3 minutes. Turn off the stovetop, slide the skillet to a cool burner, and let the mixture cool to room temperature.

CONTINUED

VIETNAMESE COCONUT TOAST
CONTINUED

6   Transfer the peanut mixture to a **mortar**. Add the salt. Use the **pestle** to roughly crush the peanut mixture. (If you don't have a mortar and pestle, add the peanut mixture and the salt to a **large zipper-lock plastic bag** and seal the bag, squeezing out as much air as possible. Use a **rolling pin** to roughly bash and crush the peanuts.)

7   Line a **rimmed baking sheet** with **aluminum foil**. Arrange the baguette slices in a single layer on the baking sheet. Place the baking sheet in the oven and bake the baguette slices until they are dried out and crisp but not browned, 1 to 3 minutes.

!! 8   Use **oven mitts** to remove the baking sheet from the oven and place it on the stovetop or a **cooling rack**. Use **tongs** to carefully flip the beautiful baguette slices over.

!! 9   Using oven mitts, return the baking sheet to the oven. Bake the baguette slices until the second side is dried out and crisp, 1 to 3 minutes. Use oven mitts to remove the baking sheet from the oven and place it on the stovetop or cooling rack.

10   Time to top the toasts. Spoon 1 teaspoon of the coconut cream mixture onto each toast (putting too much will make it soggy), sprinkle with 1 teaspoon of the shredded coconut, drizzle with 1 teaspoon of the condensed milk, and sprinkle with 1 teaspoon of the peanut mixture. (Be careful, the baking sheet will still be hot!)

!! 11   Using oven mitts, return the baking sheet to the oven. Bake until the edges of the baguette slices are gold and the coconut cream starts to bubble, 10 to 15 minutes. Remove the baking sheet from the oven and place it on the stovetop or cooling rack.

12   Now for the *fun* part! Add 4 baguette slices to each serving plate, drizzle them with a little more condensed milk, and sprinkle with a little bit more of the coconut and the peanut mixture. Serve immediately and enjoy!

Something Reyna wishes she knew when she was first learning to cook? "How much joy I would get from cooking for my family and friends."

SERVES 6

STOVETOP FALL FRUIT CRISP

INGREDIENTS

Topping

½ cup all-purpose flour

⅓ cup old-fashioned (rolled) oats

¼ cup packed brown sugar

⅛ teaspoon table salt

⅛ teaspoon ground cinnamon

4 tablespoons unsalted butter, melted (see page 17)

Filling

1 pound apples, peeled

½ pound pears, peeled

1 teaspoon lemon juice (see page 15)

1 teaspoon cornstarch

½ teaspoon Chinese five-spice powder

¼ teaspoon ground ginger

2 tablespoons packed brown sugar

Pinch of table salt

⅓ cup dried cranberries (optional)

2 tablespoons unsalted butter

Whipped cream (see page 220) or vanilla ice cream, for serving (optional)

Apples and pears are both at their tastiest in the fall. You can use any sweet, crisp apple in this recipe, such as Golden Delicious, Gala, or Honeycrisp. For pears, Bartlett, Bosc, or D'Anjou all taste great here. Be sure to use old-fashioned oats (also known as rolled oats) in this recipe (instant oats will turn to mush, and stone-ground will be tough).

1   **For the topping:** In a **medium bowl**, **whisk** the flour, oats, brown sugar, salt, and cinnamon until combined.

2   Add the melted butter and toss with a **fork** (or your fingers) until you can't see any bits of dry flour and the mixture begins to form clumps.

3   Add the topping to a **10-inch skillet**. Cook over medium-low heat, stirring often with a **rubber spatula**, until golden brown, 6 to 8 minutes.

‼4   Carefully transfer the topping to a **large plate**. Use the rubber spatula to spread it into an even layer. (No need to wash the skillet—you'll use it again in step 6.)

5   **For the filling:** Stand the peeled apples on a **cutting board** with the stems facing up. Use a **chef's knife** to slice around each apple core, cutting the apple into 4 large pieces. Discard the cores. Place each piece flat-side down on the cutting board and cut it into ½-inch-thick slices. Repeat with the peeled pears.

6   Add the lemon juice, cornstarch, five-spice powder, ginger, brown sugar, and salt to a **large bowl**. Whisk to combine. Add the apples, pears, and cranberries (if using). Stir until the fruit is well coated with the cornstarch mixture.

‼7   In the same 10-inch skillet, melt the butter over medium-low heat. Use **oven mitts** to pick up the handle of the skillet and carefully swirl the butter so it evenly coats the pan. Set the skillet back down on the stovetop.

8   Add the fruit mixture to the skillet and cook over medium-low heat, stirring occasionally with the rubber spatula, until the fruit is tender, about 15 minutes. Turn off the stovetop. Carefully slide

the skillet to a cool burner. Let the filling cool for 5 minutes.

9 Sprinkle the cooled topping over the surface of the filling. Serve warm with whipped cream or vanilla ice cream (if using).

STOVETOP CLASSIC APPLE CRISP

Use 1½ pounds apples and leave out the pears and dried cranberries. Use ground cinnamon instead of the Chinese five-spice powder.

YOU'RE THE CHEF

"The fall fruit crisp was delicious!" –Hannah, age 8

PUMPKIN CAKE WITH MAPLE GLAZE

This cake looks like a showstopper, but it's simple enough to stir together after school!

1   Set an oven rack in the middle position and heat the oven to 350°F. Spray the inside of an **8-by-8-inch square baking pan** with vegetable oil spray. Line the bottom of the pan with **parchment paper**.

2   In a **medium bowl**, **whisk** the flour, cinnamon, baking powder, baking soda, salt, and nutmeg until combined.

3   In a **large bowl**, whisk the pumpkin, brown sugar, oil, ¼ cup of the maple syrup, and eggs until well combined.

4   Add the flour mixture to the large bowl and use a **rubber spatula** to mix until just combined and you can't see any bits of dry flour.

5   Use the rubber spatula to transfer the batter to the prepared baking pan and smooth out the top.

6   Place the baking pan in the oven and bake until a toothpick inserted into the center of the cake comes out clean, 30 to 35 minutes.

7   While the cake bakes, in a **small bowl**, whisk the confectioners' sugar and remaining ¼ cup maple syrup until smooth.

!!8   Use **oven mitts** to remove the baking pan from the oven and place it on the stovetop or a **cooling rack**.

9   Let the cake cool completely in the pan, about 1½ hours. Use a **butter knife** to loosen the edges of the cake from the pan. Flip the cake out of the baking pan. Peel off and discard the parchment paper. Flip the cake right-side up onto a **serving platter** or **cutting board**.

10 Use a **spoon** to drizzle the cake with the maple glaze and toasted nuts (if using). Serve.

INGREDIENTS

Vegetable oil spray

1 cup all-purpose flour

1 teaspoon ground cinnamon

1 teaspoon baking powder

½ teaspoon baking soda

½ teaspoon table salt

¼ teaspoon ground nutmeg

1 cup unsweetened pumpkin puree

¾ cup packed light brown sugar

½ cup vegetable oil

¼ cup plus ¼ cup maple syrup, measured separately

2 large eggs

½ cup confectioners' (powdered) sugar

¼ cup chopped toasted walnuts or pecans (optional)

SERVES 4

ARROZ CON LECHE
RICE PUDDING

INGREDIENTS

½ cup long-grain
white rice

2 tablespoons unsalted
butter

2½ cups whole milk

¾ cup evaporated milk

¼ cup granulated sugar

¼ cup raisins, plus extra
for serving (optional)

1 cinnamon stick

½ teaspoon orange
zest (see page 15)

¼ teaspoon vanilla
extract

¼ teaspoon table salt

Ground cinnamon,
for serving (optional)

Versions of rice pudding are enjoyed all over the world. In Latin America, the dish is often called arroz con leche or arroz con dulce and is commonly flavored with citrus zest, evaporated milk, and/or raisins. The evaporated milk makes the pudding creamy, while the raisins, if used, become plump and tender as they cook.

1. Place a **large fine-mesh strainer** in the sink. Add the rice to the strainer. Rinse the rice under cold running water until the water runs clear, 1 to 2 minutes. Shake the strainer to drain the rice well.

2. In a **medium saucepan**, melt the butter over medium-low heat. Add the rice and cook, stirring occasionally with a **wooden spoon**, until the rice is translucent (somewhat see-through) and smells a bit nutty, about 2 minutes.

3. Add the whole milk, evaporated milk, sugar, raisins (if using), cinnamon stick, orange zest, vanilla, and salt. Stir to combine.

4. Bring the mixture to a simmer (small bubbles appear all over the surface), then reduce the heat to low. Cook, stirring occasionally with the wooden spoon, until the rice is tender and the mixture is thickened, 30 to 35 minutes. Turn off the stovetop and slide the saucepan to a cool burner.

5. Let the rice pudding cool for 10 minutes. Discard the cinnamon stick. Serve, letting everyone sprinkle their portions with extra raisins and/or ground cinnamon, if they like.

 **FUN FOOD FACT**

The orange zest in this recipe is one great use for orange peels. South African inventor Kiara Nirghin used them a little differently. She made a superabsorbent material out of orange and avocado peels that helps keep crops hydrated—even during droughts. Thanks to her innovative thinking, farmers can grow more food in dry weather.

MANGO FLOAT
FILIPINO MANGO ICEBOX CAKE

In the Philippines, this no-bake icebox-style cake is traditionally made with small, sweet, kidney-shaped Carabao or Manila mangoes. If you can find them, use them. If not, very ripe Ataulfo or Champagne mangoes are the best substitutes. Don't use frozen mango chunks—they're too tough. Plan ahead: This dessert needs to chill for at least 12 hours in the fridge before you serve it. If you want a more solid, ice cream–like treat, place the baking pan in the freezer for 1 hour before serving.

1. Place a large bowl (if using a handheld mixer) or the bowl of a stand mixer (if using) in the refrigerator to chill. (A metal bowl is ideal, if you have it.)

2. Measure the cream and condensed milk into separate liquid measuring cups. Place them in the refrigerator to chill for at least 15 minutes.

3. Meanwhile, cut the mangoes into ½-inch pieces following the photos on page 221.

4. When the bowl, cream, and condensed milk are chilled, whip the cream following the steps on page 220.

5. Add the chilled condensed milk, vanilla, and salt to the whipped cream. Whip on high speed until fully incorporated and stiff peaks form when the beaters are lifted out of the cream, 2 to 5 minutes. (To check: stop the mixer and lift the whisk or beaters out. The peaks should stand straight up and remain pointy at the top—no drooping!)

6. Add a layer of graham crackers to an 8-by-8-inch square baking pan or dish, breaking them apart as needed to fully cover the bottom of the pan (it's OK if there are small gaps or if the crackers overlap a little bit).

7. Use a rubber spatula to add one-third of the whipped cream mixture to the pan on top of the graham crackers. Spread it into an even layer. Scatter one-third of the mango pieces evenly over the cream.

CONTINUED

INGREDIENTS

2 cups heavy cream

¾ cup sweetened condensed milk

3 large, 4 medium, or 5 small very ripe mangoes (see the introduction)

½ teaspoon vanilla extract

Pinch of table salt

14 to 16 graham crackers

8   Repeat steps 6 and 7 two more times with the remaining graham crackers, whipped cream, and mango pieces, creating three layers total.

9   Cover the pan with **plastic wrap** and place it in the refrigerator. Chill for at least 12 hours and up to 24 hours. Discard the plastic wrap and use a **chef's knife** to cut the mango float into pieces. Serve on plates.

WHIPPED CREAM

Add the heavy cream to the **chilled large bowl** or the bowl of a **stand mixer**. Attach the whisk attachment to the stand mixer, if using (or use a **handheld mixer**). Whip the cream on medium-low speed until foamy bubbles form, about 1 minute. Increase the speed to high and whip until the cream is thick and you can see ripples in it, 1 to 3 minutes. (If the cream is splattering out of the bowl, drape a **clean dish towel** over the mixer and bowl to catch the drops.) Stop the mixer and lift the whisk or beaters out of the cream. If the whipped cream clings to the beaters and makes soft peaks that stand up on their own, with just a little droop at the top, it's done! If not, keep whipping and check again in 30 seconds.

YOU'RE THE CHEF
"It was refreshing, and the mangoes paired so nicely with the whipped cream and crackers. I will certainly be making this again!"
—Cali, age 15

HOW TO CUT MANGOES INTO PIECES

1

Place one mango on a cutting board, holding it with the stem facing up. Set a chef's knife just next to the stem. Slice off one half of the mango, following the curve of the pit in the center. Rotate the mango and slice off the other half. You'll be left with the long, flat pit and some mango attached to it. (Discard the pit or eat the mango flesh off of it as a snack.)

2

Use a butter knife to cut 4 to 6 lines the long way through the flesh (but not through the skin) of each mango half, about ½ inch apart. Make 6 to 8 lines the short way to create a crisscross pattern of about ½-inch squares.

3

Use your fingers to push from the skin side of the mango to pop the mango pieces outward.

4

Hold the mango half over a medium bowl. Use a spoon to scrape the mango pieces into the bowl. Repeat with the other mango half, then repeat steps 1 through 3 with the remaining mangoes. (You should have about 4 cups of mango cubes.)

BANANA "ICE CREAM"

Since this recipe uses only ONE ingredient (!), it's important that the bananas are very ripe and sweet. Look for soft bananas with heavily speckled black or brown skins. Plan ahead: You'll need to freeze the bananas for at least 8 hours before turning them into ice cream. Keep your banana ice cream simple or turn it into a sundae with homemade whipped cream (see page 220), Hot Fudge Sauce (page 228), and/or Strawberry Sauce (page 229).

1. Peel the bananas and place them on a cutting board. Use a butter knife to slice the bananas into ½-inch-thick rounds. Place the sliced bananas in a freezer bag or airtight container. Freeze until solid, at least 8 hours or overnight.

2. Remove the bananas from the freezer and add them to a food processor. Let them soften slightly, about 10 minutes.

3. Place the lid on the food processor and lock it into place. Pulse until the bananas are broken down into small crumbles, fifteen to twenty 1-second pulses.

4. Process the mixture until it's very smooth and creamy (like soft-serve ice cream), about 4 minutes, stopping the processor and using a rubber spatula to redistribute the mixture around the blade a few times during processing. If you're adding any flavorings (see page 223), add them now and process for another 30 seconds, until they're fully incorporated.

‼ 5 Stop the processor, remove the lid, and carefully remove the processor blade. Transfer the banana "ice cream" to an airtight container. You can enjoy the ice cream right away (it will be very soft) or freeze it until it's firm and scoopable, at least 4 hours or up to 5 days. Serve in little bowls.

FLAVOR YOUR BANANA "ICE CREAM"

Try adding 2 tablespoons peanut butter, honey, chocolate-hazelnut spread, or sweetened condensed milk and a pinch of ground cinnamon to the food processor at the end of step 4. (You can also look around your kitchen and come up with your own flavor inspiration!)

YOU'RE THE CHEF
"Can't believe it was just bananas—really tasted like banana ice cream!"
–Isabelle, age 8

Fany remembers strolling through Mexico City with her dad, who loved to eat food from street vendors, especially fruit sprinkled with chili powder. Sometimes he would try to hide the evidence of his snacks, but the reddish powder all over his beard would give him away.

Fany dedicated her first cookbook, *My Sweet Mexico*, to her dad. Since then, she's written three more, all inspired by the flavors of Mexico. She also runs a few different food businesses, including La Newyorkina, a catering company; Fan-Fan Doughnuts, a donut shop; and Mijo Mexican Kitchen, a food stall.

When she's cooking at home, Fany loves to share the kitchen with her five-year-old son. Together, they're working on an art project in which they write up his favorite recipes. He makes drawings and tells her the ingredients and quantities. He even has his own dinosaur apron, measuring cups, spoons, and cutters.

Fany never liked fish until she lived and worked in the seaside town of San Sebastián, Spain. The fresh seafood there changed her mind!

LONDON FOG-BERRY PALETAS

"My sister lives in London, and I miss her every day. When I was thinking of what flavor paletas to make, I really wanted to share a recipe inspired by her and where she lives. A 'London Fog' is a mix of Earl Grey tea and foamy steamed milk—it's delicious and there's something quite cozy about the Earl Grey flavor. We grew up in Mexico, and my sister is super fun and full of life, so I felt that the addition of brightly colored berries combined with the creamy London Fog would show off a bit of her personality and how I feel when I am with her." —Fany Gerson

INGREDIENTS

London Fog–Cream Layer

¾ cup heavy cream

¾ cup whole milk

6 tablespoons granulated sugar

2 teaspoons loose-leaf Earl Grey tea (from 2 tea bags)

½ teaspoon vanilla extract

Pinch of salt

Berry-Honey Layer

¾ cup raspberries, blueberries, or blackberries, fresh or frozen

1 tablespoon honey

1½ teaspoons confectioners' (powdered) sugar

⅓ cup water

Pinch of salt

½ teaspoon lemon or lime juice (see page 15)

1. **For the London Fog–cream layer:** In a **small saucepan**, combine the cream, milk, sugar, tea, vanilla, and salt. Cook over medium heat, stirring occasionally with a **wooden spoon**, until the mixture comes to a simmer (small bubbles appear all over the surface). Turn off the stovetop and cover the saucepan with a lid. Let the tea steep for 15 to 20 minutes.

‼ 2. Place a **large liquid measuring cup** or **bowl with a spout** in the sink. Set a **fine-mesh strainer** over the liquid measuring cup. Carefully strain the tea mixture into the liquid measuring cup. Let the mixture cool to room temperature, about 1 hour.

3. **Meanwhile, for the berry-honey layer:** In a **clean small saucepan**, combine the berries, honey, confectioners' sugar, water, and salt. Cook over medium heat, stirring occasionally with a **clean wooden spoon**, until the sugar has dissolved, the berries are broken down, and the mixture is slightly thick, 8 to 10 minutes. Turn off the stovetop.

‼ 4. Carefully transfer the berry mixture to a **blender** (be careful—it's hot!). Let the mixture cool until it's just warm, about 30 minutes. Add the lemon juice. Place the lid on top of the blender, hold it in place with a folded **kitchen towel**, and blend until the mixture is smooth, about 30 seconds. Stop the blender.

CONTINUED

LONDON FOG–BERRY PALETAS
CONTINUED

5 Set the fine-mesh strainer over a second liquid measuring cup or bowl with a spout. Carefully transfer the berry mixture to the strainer. Use a rubber spatula to stir and press the mixture through the strainer. Discard any solid bits left behind in the strainer.

6 Divide the berry-honey mixture evenly among six ice pop molds, followed by the London Fog mixture (leave a little bit of room at the top of each mold—the liquid will expand as it freezes). Use a skewer or chopstick to lightly swirl the two mixtures, though this might happen naturally as you pour.

7 Freeze the paletas until they're solid, 5 to 6 hours. Once the paletas are fully solid, dip the molds into warm water covering the sides, unmold, and enjoy!

NO ICE POP MOLDS? NO PROBLEM!

In step 6, instead of ice pop molds, you can use six 3-ounce paper cups. Once you've added and swirled the two layers, cover each cup with a small piece of aluminum foil. Use a paring knife to make a small slit in the middle of the foil. Insert a wooden ice pop stick into each slit in the foil, so the sticks are standing straight up. Continue with the recipe in step 7.

Fany's first cookbook won a James Beard award, a high honor for chefs and food writers.

HOT FUDGE SAUCE

INGREDIENTS

½ cup granulated sugar

⅓ cup half-and-half

¼ cup unsweetened cocoa powder

6 tablespoons semisweet chocolate chips

2 tablespoons unsalted butter

½ teaspoon vanilla extract

¼ teaspoon ground cinnamon (optional)

⅛ teaspoon table salt

This rich, chocolaty topping is easier to make than you might expect. If you're reheating leftover hot fudge sauce, be careful not to heat it for too long, or the sauce will separate. Drizzle your sauce over Banana "Ice Cream" (page 222) or your favorite store-bought frozen dessert.

1. Add all the ingredients to a small saucepan.

2. Cook over medium-low heat, stirring constantly with a rubber spatula, until the chocolate is melted and the sauce is smooth, about 5 minutes.

3. Turn off the heat. Carefully slide the saucepan to a cool burner. Let the sauce cool for 5 minutes. Serve warm. (You can store leftover hot fudge sauce in an airtight container in the refrigerator for up to 1 month. Before serving, reheat the sauce in the microwave, stirring every 10 seconds, until it's smooth and pourable.)

 FUN FOOD FACT

When Erin Hamlin, an Olympic medalist in luge, won her first world championship medal, the ice cream shop in her hometown of Remsen, New York, named a sundae after her. It was made with Oreos, peanut butter, peanut butter cups, whipped cream, and, of course, hot fudge sauce.

STRAWBERRY SAUCE

Drizzle this sweet sauce over Banana "Ice Cream" (page 222), Chocolate Sheet Cake (page 202), Mini German Pancakes (page 45), or Classic French Toast (page 38). There's no need to thaw the berries before starting to cook. You can use frozen mixed berries instead of the frozen strawberries, or you can use fresh strawberries—you'll have to hull and chop them first, and reduce the cooking time in step 1 to 3 to 4 minutes.

INGREDIENTS

2 cups frozen strawberries

⅓ cup granulated sugar

2 teaspoons lemon juice (see page 15)

1   In a **medium saucepan**, combine the frozen strawberries, sugar, and lemon juice. Cook on the stovetop over medium heat, stirring occasionally with a **wooden spoon** or **rubber spatula**, until the sugar has dissolved and the mixture is bubbling all over, 7 to 9 minutes.

2   Reduce the heat to medium-low and cook, stirring occasionally, until the berries are very soft, about 5 minutes.

3   Turn off the stovetop and slide the saucepan to a cool burner. Let the sauce cool for 5 minutes.

4   Use a **potato masher** to mash the berries in the saucepan until they're broken down (be careful, the saucepan will still be hot). Serve warm. (You can store leftover strawberry sauce in an airtight container in the refrigerator for up to 1 week. Before serving, reheat the sauce in the microwave, stirring every 10 seconds, until it's pourable.)

 REBEL IN THE KITCHEN

Leah Chase grew up on her family's strawberry farm in Louisiana. When she got older, she became an iconic award-winning chef and civil rights activist—and the inspiration for Tiana in Disney's *The Princess and the Frog*. After she died in 2019, her grandchildren took over her New Orleans restaurant, the fourth generation in the family to run it.

ACKNOWLEDGMENTS

Rebel Girls would like to acknowledge all the chefs who contributed recipes! Thank you for sharing your stories, memories, and recipes with us.

Ali Slagle	Hetty Lui McKinnon
Ana Sortun	Lauren Toyota
Andi Oliver	Portia Mbau
Andrea Nguyen	Priya Krishna
Asma Khan	Rahanna Bisseret Martinez
Eva Chin	Reyna Dương
Fany Gerson	Sarah Thomas

Rebel Girls would like to acknowledge all the Rebels who helped us test these recipes—and their families, too! Thank you for sharing your thoughts about food and your kitchen adventures with us.

Addy	Goldie	Maya
Anastasia	Halle	Olivia
Arden	Isabelle	Pierce
Ariana	J	Place
Astrid	Lara	Robyn
Cali	Liliya	Saanya
Charlie	Linnea	Sophie
Coco	Luka	Taj
Ella	Madison	Viva
Etta	Malia	Vivian
Evie	Marian	Yelena

And finally, special thanks to the Rebel Girls team: Amy Pfister, Eliza Kirby, Giulia Flamini, Hannah Bennett, Jes Wolfe, Jess Harriton, Jessica Novak, Kristen Brittain, Michon Vanderpoel, Rachel Toby, Sarah Parvis, Taleen Alexander-Houck

ABOUT REBEL GIRLS

Rebel Girls, a certified B Corporation, is a global, multi-platform empowerment brand dedicated to helping raise the most inspired and confident generation of girls through content, experiences, products, and community. Originating from an international bestselling children's book, Rebel Girls amplifies stories of real-life, extraordinary women throughout history, geography, and field of excellence. With a growing community of 35 million self-identified Rebel Girls spanning more than 100 countries, the brand engages with Generation Alpha through its book series, premier app and audio content, events, and merchandise. To date, Rebel Girls has sold more than 11 million books in 50 languages and reached 55 million audio listens. Award recognition includes the *New York Times* bestseller list, the 2022 Apple Design Award for Social Impact, multiple Webby Awards for Family, Kids & Education, and Common Sense Media Selection honors, among many others.

As a B Corp, we're part of a global community of businesses that meet high standards of social and environmental impact.

JOIN THE REBEL GIRLS COMMUNITY!

Visit rebelgirls.com and join our email list for exclusive sneak peeks, promos, activities, and more. You can also email us at hello@rebelgirls.com.

YouTube: youtube.com/RebelGirls

App: rebelgirls.com/audio

Podcast: rebelgirls.com/podcast

Facebook: facebook.com/rebelgirls

Instagram: @rebelgirls

Email: hello@rebelgirls.com

Web: rebelgirls.com

If you liked this book, please take a moment to review it wherever you prefer!

MORE FROM REBEL GIRLS!

Let stories about real-life women and girls entertain and inspire you.

Enjoy interactive books and gifts!

Find helpful advice and Q&As between tweens and experts in the Growing Up Powerful series.

Read letters, poems, essays, and more from 145 extraordinary teens and women.

Dig deeper into the lives of five real-life heroines with the Rebel Girls chapter book series.

Go on an incredible middle-grade adventure with *Nina and the Mysterious Mailbox.*

PLUS! LISTEN TO REBEL GIRLS STORIES

Scan to hear exciting stories about extraordinary women and girls from all around the world and throughout history.

INDEX

Note: Page references in *italics* indicate photographs.

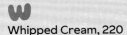
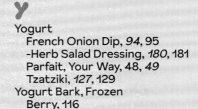

Published in the United States by Ten Speed Press, an imprint of the
Crown Publishing Group, a division of Penguin Random House LLC, New York.
TenSpeed.com

Ten Speed Press and the Ten Speed Press colophon are registered trademarks
of Penguin Random House LLC.

Typefaces: Colophon Foundry's Sunset Gothic, Studio Funshop's Goops & Kooky
Cloud, Hanoded's Crowd Pleaser, Forth and Wild's Furry Friend

Library of Congress Cataloging-in-Publication Data
Names: Rebel Girls, editor.
Title: Rebel Girls cook : 100+ kid-tested recipes you can make, share, and enjoy! /
Rebel Girls.
Identifiers: LCCN 2023052912 (print) | LCCN 2023052913 (ebook) | ISBN
9780593835579 (hardcover) | ISBN 9780593835586 (ebook)
Subjects: LCSH: Cooking—Juvenile literature. | Cooking for children—Juvenile literature. |
LCGFT: Cookbooks.
Classification: LCC TX652.5 .R43 2024 (print) | LCC TX652.5 (ebook) | DDC 641.5/123--dc23/
eng/20240126
LC record available at https://lccn.loc.gov/2023052912
LC ebook record available at https://lccn.loc.gov/2023052913

Hardcover ISBN: 978-0-593-83557-9
eBook ISBN: 978-0-593-83558-6

Printed in China

Textured backgrounds by TITUS GROUP; hand-drawn arrows arrows by svetolk, Sunil, and
Lysenko.A — stock.adobe.com

Acquiring editor: Molly Birnbaum | Project editor: Kristin Sargianis |
Production editor: Joyce Wong | Editorial assistant: Gabby Ureña Matos
Designer: Annie Marino | Art director: Emma Campion
Production designers: Mari Gill and Faith Hague
Production manager & prepress color manager: Jane Chinn
Food stylist: Carrie Ann Purcell
Food stylist assistants: Daniela Swamp, Max Rappaport
Prop stylist: Hina Mistry
Photo assistants: Ashli Buts, David Koung, Dave Klaus
Recipe developers: Afton Cyrus, Andrea Rivera Wawrzyn
Copyeditor: Andrea Peabbles
Proofreader: Ivy McFadden | Indexer: Elizabeth Parson
Publicist: Kristin Casemore | Marketer: Andrea Patronova

10 9 8 7 6 5 4 3 2 1

First Edition